The Invention of Violence

▼

Short Fiction by Douglas Gunn

CINCO PUNTOS PRESS
El Paso • Texas

ACKNOWLEDGEMENTS

Grateful acknowledgement is given to the following publications in which a number of these stories first appeared: *Caliban* ("the woman and the cop" which was published as "police brutality"); *Boundary 2* ("a living"); *Another Chicago Magazine* ("physical therapy"); *Tyuonyi* ("class consciousness," "agonistics," "Not Rich," and "Gun Control").

The story "watching movies" was in Douglas Gunn's first collection of stories, a*nd working* (Permanent Press, London, 1991).

ISBN 0-938317-22-9
Library of Congress Number 94-073944

FIRST EDITION

Special thanks to Steve Brown
Cover photograph by Richard Baron
Book design, cover design and typography by Vicki Trego Hill
Type is set in Adobe Garamond and Binner Gothic
Printed on acid free paper
by McNaughton & Gunn of Saline, Michigan

NATIONAL
ENDOWMENT
FOR THE
ARTS

This book is funded in part
by generous support from
the National Endowment for the Arts.

The
Invention
of
Violence

To Justin,

May this book shepard you through good times and bad times, happiness and sorrow, felicity and desperation. Thanks for the Chronic,

—Allison & Zack

Contents

▼

▼

To Stefan & Emma

The
Invention
of
Violence

Some Things You Can Do As a Last Resort

▼

1. Taking Advantage of a Bad Situation

IT WAS A TIME he would
spend his days getting the paper and in the kitchen and the want-
ads, classifieds about a job. It went for a number of months like
this, the pressure of getting there in time for a job, several months
like it, but his wife had a job but she didn't make enough as a
waitress and they didn't have enough. A résumé didn't seem to
help, he had a good one prepared by an agency and with his
qualifications it wasn't hard to make it look impressive, but
paying the bills, and long-distance phone calls were too much: he
wouldn't say anything but she called her parents every month. But
it was her paying the phone bills and wasn't worth it if she would
point this out, being supported was the term, but it was the
economy and he knew other men in the same or similar circumstances, this helped if they were his friends, and thousands of
others but the problem of it wouldn't go away inside his marriage.

He said look, I'll try for something else. It meant not as much money but it meant the feeling of being supported by your wife, it would go away. It was too bad, because of his years of experience wasted and in the long term a bad choice for his career but something to do was the important thing to save his marriage.

His wife came in here in a surprising way though, and it takes him by surprise but she simply says no. It's a shock that makes him speechless, with the pressures of finding a job and the responsibility of the house, etc., because seeing the logic of it (the long term and more money and a better job) but the implication that the authority of a husband is money but she makes the money, it gives her the right to say it. He says wait a minute, he says what are you: a waitress. A couple days are spent in silence, as a husband he doesn't know how to cope with this latest development or he can't think of a way to accept a new attitude of his wife, and she won't admit it but he knows she's taking advantage of a bad situation, the economy again. No communication is finally possible, he leaves, the excuse is he'll go to another city with his resume, his bag is packed and he tells her this, a kiss on the cheek and he opens the door. He goes, and a room is out of the question because of the money, the decision is between a cousin and a room in the YMCA. Briefly, he considers a homeless shelter, it wouldn't be so bad but it wouldn't be fair: he has a home. The cousin is someone he likes, although they don't know each other well any more but he'd ask too many questions and want to know too much. It's the Y, then, any little job will support him here or a temporary agency, and he won't use up the money he brought and he can get a room with a bath for five dollars a day more. Something will have to be done about a real job though and getting his marriage back on track, if this is what it takes. Why else is he here.

A Chinese man with one arm takes his money and checks

him in, sleeve folded up, lovely friendly man, fifties, and a wife is in the background with cleaning supplies, but she doesn't look up but she says something in Chinese, he assumes it's Chinese. It's a good living, to run the YMCA, not your own little hotel and you could always lose your job to hard times but you could lose your place too, if you had a place. And they look comfortable, a living quarter, he sees the signs of it through a door behind the counter, and like they've been there for years, the idea that they're settled in. The one-armed man tells him he can use the facilities, pool and weight room, gym, and makes him feel at home, because of the friendliness and it eases his mind: it's not out of the question, any number of single men live like this, worse. He has to go outside to get to his room, metal steps to a door on the second floor, inside and up more steps to the third floor, a door, then the hall. The Chinese man gives him keys to all these doors and to his room, dirty but its the bed that bothers him, soft. It's worse than he expected but it has a window that opens to control the heat and you can see a basketball court outside, but it has a rug with the nap worn away and stains and stains on the walls and on the ceiling. In the hall a man was holding a portable tv and knocked on the door next to his, softly knocking.

2. Against Her Better Judgement

A GIRL CAME FROM THE SUBURBS of the Sunbelt, grass would grow in the yards, from the sprinkler systems and green from fertilizer and the people had front and back yards and space between the ranch houses they lived in, bushes on the side but enough grass to mow on the side too. Sidewalks were white cement and wide streets, cars parked on each side left room for cars to pass in both directions, slowly because of children and balls would roll into the street from slanted driveways, with their windows rolled up for the air conditioning. It seemed like Arizona, or a suburb in California. 14, and the girl was living with her father because the mother died suddenly some time ago, or the mother was gone, it's not clear. Relatives lived in the town, sisters of the father, and the father wore a tie to work each day and the father came home but often he didn't and the girl didn't know where he was. He watched tv sitting in a chair and smoked cigarettes, the house smelled like it but he would gargle Listerine from the bottle, tobacco smoke and the smell of disinfectant, and she remembered him shaving his armpits. The daughter was expected to cook and the dishes had to be washed, etc., and seemed frightened inside herself. Or she might have felt isolated. The school bus for the high school and the middle school, when it stopped on the corner in her neighborhood with the red lights flashing and the girl stood alone in a group waiting for it and looked like she needed something done with her hair, washing it would help. Probably she was sexually abused, it was the father and there was nowhere to turn. The possibility of drugs was good, pills you couldn't smell, with others at school or after school because the father wasn't around and it was an escape, the help-lessness of abuse. She was too terrified to know how far it went, or she couldn't say exactly what happened and her mother was dead, she couldn't turn to the sisters. Of course, there are shelters or something like a home where you can go in this kind of crisis but she didn't know about it, a distant relative was her only hope, an uncle who wasn't aware of any of this, she ran away vaguely in his direction.

She got far away hitch-hiking, short rides from locals took her to beyond the edge of town and she lied about herself and her home to a woman, who made her promise to go to a shelter in another town and took her there, the woman said it was on her way, and said it was good that it was her happened along and not someone to hurt the girl. The woman watched the girl go in the door of the shelter and drove off and the girl left. She hitch-hiked some more to a junction far from the edge of town and waited there a long time, three hours, and cars would pass her by, occasional cars kept passing her, and her pleading with them as they passed, aloud in her voice or shout her plea as they passed and finally had to simply cry as it began to get dark, tears on her cheeks mixed with dirt from the road and made her look pathetic like a child would and she still was one, a child and too young for the terror of the road and night on the road.

Finally a man stopped in a pickup, she didn't want to but she got in, the idea that a man might be dangerous and a cruel man could be driving a pickup from a ranch with ranch hands, women weren't respected, girls weren't, and they might be cruel to you. The man watched her get in and you could say he looked dangerous with dirty hands and needed a shave, etc., but he wasn't, and felt sorry for the girl, a ranch hand that knew how women were sometimes treated by his friends and men he worked with, but with a wife, and his wife was pregnant and they knew from the tests it was a girl. The girl didn't tell him anything so he didn't have to imagine something about himself but he thought of his own daughter in 14 years and would she run away or would she be alone, or would she be alone on the road. The man was at home by himself while the wife visited a sister briefly, and considering this he said, do you have any money. She said no.

He could afford a room in the YMCA and he registered her there and because he knew the Chinese man and knew he'd be curious and his wife would be curious but there wouldn't be the questions you might expect, he knew this. He took the girl to her room and took her in her room, she didn't have any suitcase but she couldn't make it up the stairs and he carried her in his arms, he laid her down on the bed and she was immediately sleeping, he watched her and then he left asking the Chinese man and his wife to pay attention to her, if she tried to leave or needed help, and went home to get something, or to consider what he should do.

3. Steady Work

ON THE FLOOR, the carpet worn thin over wood made an ideal surface for the point of Bob's dagger when it went in when he played a version of mumbledy-peg, from laying on his bed, and bored, and nothing to do. He wanted to watch game shows or an occasional soap-opera but the pawn shop tv broke down after he could watch anything he wanted for a week that it worked. It was four days ago and even if he stayed up as late as he could find something to do he couldn't sleep past two or sometimes one, and had six or seven hours until time to go to Jay's or sometimes Lucy's and something would begin. Money wasn't a problem, from his job, but it was possible to use some of this time getting rid of something or picking up extra cash for something but Bob had time on his hands no matter how long this took and the money was in his pocket for another day or two. Until he shipped out there was a week ten days, Chicago Trader, deckhand and a regular job if he didn't pick up something at the union hall first, he might go down there but it was sitting around and he didn't need to. It was a month on and a month off and if he could be patient he could have the same job back, and sometimes they would call him sooner or sometimes he could work past his month. There was a substantial sum of money involved but he was the kind of individual to keep up his child support and two ex-wives and kids, it took most of it. Occasionally he'd take something on another boat from impatience but it was risking it that someone else would take his regular job and that it would take a number of rotations to get it back. The job was making tow in the canals and the Illinois River runs through Joliet, barges would be loaded and waiting at various locations to add to the tow, locks, breaking the tow in various ways, the different levels and you put it back together on the other side, it depends on the size of the lock. The point was to get it through but you had to get it apart and back together and the faster the better, others were waiting to use the lock, other tow-boats and some with tows waiting in a line and each was assigned a time. He could make lead-man because he knew the best ways but he didn't want it, rather work the cables and he didn't need the money, ratchet tight the cables that tie together the barges and didn't have to think ahead to the locks or the grain elevators and where various barges would be dropped and the ways to string the barges to break them apart. Building tow on the way through Joliet and South Chicago where industry is and this is what you trade for another tow from the south where it came to be sorted out and dropped off, 30 barges, breaking a barge loose when you strike the wires and you did it with the sound of metal, the smell of metal and rust. You can feel the rust. He missed it and wanted to feel it, and the activity of pulling on a one-inch cable until it's taut and reaches the chain links at the end of a ratchet or stringing out the running lights at night, they get tangled but there's a satisfaction even in that if you know how.

But he couldn't and he couldn't watch tv. He flipped his knife in the air and it came down and stuck in the floor where he could reach it. He reached down and pulled it out and flipped it up, he was counting the times the knife flipped in the air before sticking. He pulled it out and all of a sudden he threw the knife across the room and watched it flipping around three times before it stuck its point in the window frame, it looked like three. You could tell he'd done this before because there were a number of other knife marks there where he'd pulled it out of the window frame in the past. But it didn't help and he got up and left the knife stuck in the window frame, to get ready to pick up Jay for Lucy's, pulled on his jeans and a black sweater, and putting some things in his pockets and it seemed like there was a sound like the tv was on. But this couldn't be right because he heard the sound but it was from the wrong place, stopping and realizing that a neighbor in a nearby room had a tv and just turned something on, a show and he recognized faintly the theme song of a game show he liked to watch. He was surprised someone else had a tv on his floor because it was something new and made him decide to pick up the little tv in his room, why keep a broken tv. He did and carried it easily to the door of his room and went down to the lobby to give the little tv to the man who ran the place. But no one was behind the counter, little window actually, where you fill out the card when you register and pay the money. This is where Bob left the tv on the counter, he knew the man would appreciate it even if it was broken, these people could do miracles and fix any electric thing. Bob was a good tenant, paid for his room by the month and kept his room even when he was on the boat.

4. He Couldn't Place It

THERE WERE NO JOBS, he'd been out only twice with his resume, place to place that might consider hiring him or looking at it and not many would, but he was too discouraged to continue with it, and staying in a strange city was depressing at the YMCA and homeless people would wander the streets and some would ask him for money or change and he gave them more than he felt he could afford. He didn't call but he had a round trip bus ticket and it was time to use it to get back, without knowing what he could say or what they would talk about or say about his decision to leave or coming back and it made him anxious, to think about it, he didn't want to but he didn't want to stay and if he went home it meant figuring out something to say about it. But he had to if he wanted to be home, he lived there too. He went in time to sit in a bar and he had money and spent it on beer, enough time for several beers and didn't stop drinking them until he realized the bus would leave, and forgot his suitcase in his panic to catch it, pretty drunk but he made the bus in time but there was no time to go back for the suitcase and he didn't ask, the bus was pulling out. He took a seat and the bus wasn't full because of the recession people couldn't afford to travel, and found a seat by himself. He was drunk, and the lost suitcase, that bothered him, but soon he had another beer hidden in his coat, and drank it, it turned his mind to his wife, the waitress, and tips were not as good but with a salary that could sustain them if their relationship and the love of a marriage could somehow mend or if you could get it back. This is where the beer took over and it brought him back to a feeling of frustration, or why should he have to be in a position of apologizing if he was being supported, wasn't he working, to get something and get back on track? It wasn't easy to answer if you were drunk especially but it would have to do, he turned his attention to the twilight scenery and let the beer take over his senses and his mind could take a break. The bus picked up speed, leaving the area and the industry of the outskirts of a major urban area but the bus stopped and he didn't know why, slowed and stopped and they were all straining their necks and finally he saw a river and a bridge was raising to let barges go by and a line of traffic was backed up in front of the bus and you could see their red tail lights in the dusk. It probably made him think of something else, it should be about the television but he couldn't remember something and it bothered him in his mind like a dream, but he couldn't place it.

Paul
& Me

▼

1987

THEY WERE TALKING ABOUT something but he didn't know why or what they kept talking about, all of it, or if they would have to if it would be resolved, somehow. An idea would improve something but their job was to work out the discrepancies, John tried to imagine the motivation for an idea at first, but a meeting was important and it was to talk about these things, they had to be ideas. The skills involved were developed over the course of a number of years and the careers of men and women, literally hundreds of years between them because some were old. They would retire, he saw this and something like this would often amaze him, age, and a young man couldn't imagine the years it takes to develop these positions and the ways to concede and when to insist on it. The first question was intention, or they called it philosophy as a college committee and they were the professors, or they could use the word politics, some preferred it. It was the benefit of the individual student or education in general, the abstract, they should be the same and the job of the professors was to decide. Ideas were good but better if you had a reason as an educator, self-interest was bad, John understood this much, they were sincere and some wore ties and white shirts, he was wearing his tie but you could loosen it but you left it on, you didn't want to lose a tie, if you would take it off and forget where you put it. What if you took someone else's tie. But the language of it took some more time, so a student could understand it, a comma should be in the right place, it affects meaning, a conjunction, ambiguity and it brings up the question of intention again, if a student would read it. Politics was the implication, if you don't simply omit a comma, why shouldn't it be it's important. It is important, but doesn't it mean something. Does it mean it to a student. John begins to wonder about little kids, his and if the others have kids, when they go to bed if anyone wants to see them tonight. Of course, it's inappropriate, but he wouldn't say anything because he doesn't know if he should make his first-grader go to bed, when he should. Just say it in two sentences: John was a new professor of English Literature so he knew this much about a comma, to make a contribution. A joke was made: it was his "domain" but he learned something, that this contribution meant he'd volunteered to write it up, a final version of the committee and the proposal, it was "hammered out" in subcommittees and meetings and various memos and responses to what they had to say (they xeroxed them and saved them in a folder or their desk drawer, there was no charge), revisions to change something and put them in the mailboxes of committee members. Of course, he would and felt glad to find a way to be recognized, it demonstrates you're willing to assume responsibility, he was careful to and he pretended to follow it but couldn't, what was different or if it was worth it, this discussion and people representing so many hundreds of years, their time, and the world-series games you could be watching. But he had the notes, he thought he'd write it so it would look like it but wouldn't

change the substance of the original version of it, to see if you
could notice. Or reverse it: you can't detect a difference but it is, it
looks exactly the same though. But it was a new job, in a Department, large state university etc., meant you had to be careful to
look serious because of "tenure." It would be a joke but out of
the question because he couldn't risk fucking up, probation like a
new worker, boilermaker's union in a shipyard, six months: but it
had another name and it was five years. A boilermaker can listen
to Paul Harvey *News and Comment*, John shaves every morning
and there's a radio in the bathroom, he makes sure he gets up
earlier than his kids and his wife before the noise starts, he likes
the way he says his words. He used to make his kids be quiet for
it but not anymore.

1978

ONCE HE WOULD GO EARLY TO WORK, 6:30, and they were a two
car family, John drove the second car to work, with rust and
the passenger door wouldn't shut but it didn't matter for work,
automatic transmission and it had an AM radio. It was a half-
hour to himself in the car with a thermos of hot coffee and the
morning newspaper before the others arrived, he already wore
bifocals for reading articles in the paper, and Paul Harvey would
come on and he would listen to it and listen to morning radio
when it was over. Old Max came early too, sometimes, but stayed
in his beat up car if he didn't come with his friend and John
stayed in his car. He liked to keep up on the news but he had to
have this time to relax, it was a way of preparing for the day
mentally and he did it by being alone. The job was framing
houses and John was young, before he could decide on a "second
career," sometimes you work in an industry or construction,
assembly line or outside in any weather and there was no reason

to think of other possibilities. With a pregnant wife it was a good job, a 28 oz. framing axe made his hands raw with blisters in high school, but they healed and calluses toughened them, now it was a job to support a wife and he had the skill to swing the axe, set a sixteen penny nail then drive it home with a single blow, depending on the wood two or three. You frame the walls flat on the floor, framing square and lay out the top- and bottom-plates tacked together then separate them, spread the studs out, by dropping an armful that tumbles and rattles and arrange them where they go and a foot, workboot, holds the stud in place against the plate and set a nail, or you can set them both because your left hand is a handful of nails. Set a sixteen penny nail, the framing axe up, is balanced at the top, and rise slightly at the waist on the down-stroke, the waffled head a perfect angle drives the nailhead into the soft two-by-four that bleeds the moisture it collects from the dew of each morning, imprint of the face of the axe and the sound it makes. When he was a kid and John lived with his grandmother, a new house just built in a subdivision and men building houses all around his grandmother's house and the constant syncopation of hammers, he could see the hammer strike across the street and the sound echoes a second later. Two nails, move on to the next stud. A wall is fifteen feet long is done in ten minutes. Someone cuts-in a sway-brace behind him, set the depth on the skill-saw and you just trace the diagonal of the one-by you'll use first, with a pencil, or he does it himself if no one else does, sometimes they simply use a four-by-eight sheet of plywood at the outside corners, it's the same thickness as black celatex, close enough. Halfway through the morning a ten-minute break and it stops, the activity and the sounds of his job and John is isolated in it, but he sits down it's quiet with the others, on a piece of two-by-four because sitting on the cement gives you hemorrhoids, Ernie is the boss and says this whenever a new man joins the crew. They sit and lean against the studs of framed walls, finding a corner is best, the others would try to think of things to talk about, sports (including hunting and fishing) or the job, houses they had just finished or what was next. Do they have another slab poured for us, yes but the plumber's not ready for us, I thought he was supposed to be out of there, he was supposed to be. Or something about the roofers, you could always smell their tar. John tried to think of something to say, he could say something about the job but Emilio had more experience and he felt stupid if it was something obvious about materials or a question about framing the roof, Emilio would say things and he wouldn't understand, he pretended he understood but you had to be careful, he didn't want to fall off a top-plate if it wasn't tied in because of something Emilio said. Once he went to Emilio's house, wife and a little kid and he supported his mother and younger brothers in a little house in the valley, stucco walls and kids' dirty hands made them shiny, and pencil marks, or broken tiles missing from the tile floors. He sat in the kitchen and Emilio had a huge smile, you could see the gums above his top teeth and bloodshot eyes, gave him a beer and sat down with him and had a beer but there was a lot of shouting and noise, Emilio kept yelling something at his little kid about running in and out and shouting at his wife to make him stop, they didn't have to talk about anything. John felt embarrassed and he left after a beer, but he felt bad because Emilio said something to his brother about him in Spanish and they laughed, he could guess what it was.

1972

HE THOUGHT PAUL HARVEY WAS STUPID, he thought he acted like a jerk when his father would listen to him, or he was always on in the background in the kitchen, but his father said

John was critical of everything. He had his own room, he went there, he had his own radio. His father acted like a jerk too, working in a shop repairing radiators and spent the weekend drinking beer and watching football on TV, at work he listened to the Country Western station, the one at home. It was a big shop, a company of diesel trucks, repairing and servicing diesel trucks that were brought in by the truckers that owned them or trucking companies owned them sometimes but the truckers brought them in and the shop had a contract to service them. It sounds like servicing horses: what's your father do he services truckers. But it was an extremely old shop, to be able to remember if it wasn't, ever, and that you could watch his father lower a radiator into the enormous vat of water to find the leak with one of the block-and-tackles lined up over a row of open tanks where they worked, they had metal lids on hinges but they were always open with a chain, steam came out. Each had a button to push, green to lower or red to raise the radiator and a torch was in a holder by each tank burning a small flame, he could see why it could be called licking. This seemed to be for solder and he saw them turn the flame up to a blue flame to clean out the old solder from time to time also, banging it with a mallet and while they stood there on a greasy boardwalk raised—black from carbon not greasy—above where the water would always spill out, in their greasy workboots. Black radiators and radiator belts that were hanging around the walls of the shop, for years and things he couldn't identify black from carbon soot smoke from the torches and the water in the tanks was green from antifreeze and oil floated on top. John would drive down and have lunch with his father from time to time if he had a day off from school in the bar next door, where they knew him from a little kid when he visited his father at work even then, but it was with his mother. This is where he first saw his father without teeth, the bathroom of this bar and where they both went to take a leak, he turned and his father was grinning at him with his gums, John had to sit down on the floor of the bathroom from laughing so hard he couldn't stop, his father said it's a good thing you finished taking a leak. It was a good joke and he told his friend at high school and his friend didn't think it was dumb but he didn't get how funny it was, it was best to drop it. But it got hard, getting hard because they both started recently suspecting their parents were jerks, Paul Harvey again and John wondered if he should say something about it but it was a good thing because he found out his friend would listen to Paul Harvey with his parents, and agreed with it. He said don't be so hard on your parents, John didn't think it was that, obviously his friend was trying to be a good friend but it was best to forget about it, parents for a couple more years, to think about science, where mice were multiplying in a lab behind the biology room making a lot of work cleaning their cages and the data they collected for a DNA experiment after school. It would help them get into a good college, if it worked, to get out of the little southern town in East Texas it was the first step, a job would come later and he agreed, his father said it was bad to end up in a radiator shop, he never would. The idea was to make money as an engineer, a scholarship was first. There was the question of what to do with the mice, you inject them and do certain tests after a prescribed amount of time, etc., the time in an activity maze, how many squares do they enter, and then the question of disposing of them. It was easily solved when his friend's younger brother mentioned someone with a snake, certain snake owners were always looking for food if the snake liked its food alive, and there seemed to be a network of people who did. They took the mice to them and made a little cash from it, even, and got them into a good college, standing in college with his father in a large city in the Midwest the first day of college, freshman orientation is next and his father says what

are you going to major in, he already knew but John saw he
wanted to ask a question about his son in college, it made him
glad his father did. Science was hard in college, though, calculus,
physics, he quit, a girl was pregnant.

1990

THEY DON'T FIRE YOU but they don't "renew your contract," and
this is how he lost his job, they can fire you and call it something else, a "line" disappears. Cf: "pack up your tools!" Pack up
your tools, a line has disappeared. The implication was politics
because of his good record as a teacher with a good "professional
profile," articles and wrote a chapter for a publisher that liked it
for a book and a good "service" record, it was politics because he
couldn't get along with a woman with power in the department.
If a student said he hated her John didn't like to but it was gratify-
ing, and his problem was trying to talk to a person who denied
something as obvious as a change like that: they were on good
terms, supportive when she read his "work" and they "shared a
critical perspective" that others respected and others envied his
professional relationship with a person with her reputation but
suddenly it disappeared, another friend was on a committee to
evaluate a graduate student's oral exam in a room, and John was
and the woman was and the student was there, you choose your
committee. He wasn't sure how it happened or what his friend
asked about something to make the woman put the student in the
middle, it was subtle enough to make the student defensive and
he was extremely uneasy, John tried to help him out with a
question about a text but the woman said why don't you compare
the essay's influence. The student was not at all sure of himself
because of his nervousness, John knew this and the others knew it
but he also knew the woman had resisted a dialog and insisted on

this performance and it was a pretty good performance, considering. It lasted a long time, two hours and the main thing was not said because it was between the woman and John's friend and they said it when they talked to the student, sometimes John seemed to but it was irrelevant. She said "how do you avoid the appearance of complicity," the question of H.'s politics, the implication was the student's dissertation and H.'s "thought," recent rumors about his political "sympathies." Of course it was wildly exaggerated and she knew this but it meant John's friend had to think of a way to respond (or John could but he was "out of his league"). Finally the student passed, they shook his hand but afterwards his friend apologized in John's office, and he was never sure why something changed, it was the deterioration of a relationship with a powerful person, his friend was powerful but he couldn't make a line reappear. And John felt naive but he would be direct and the woman would never admit something was different. He came home and gave the news of the missing line to his wife, and thinking about a job as a carpenter again (1978) or a boilermaker, something else and thinking about any job in something that isn't academic, it was not a good time for the neighbor's dog to bark all evening, you're considering another change in a career. Finally he went outside and found a rock to throw, pissed off and he jumped up to get it over the high fence at the dog, throwing it and came down off balance twisting his ankle bad, enough to limp home on the other foot with the swelling already like a baseball, sink into a chair and ice, his wife took care of this. But he felt better, in the morning he heard a story about a boy who was feeding a pig and the pig tore the boy's arms off on Paul Harvey, he dialed the phone with his teeth, a pencil.

the
overnight
visit

▼

I SHOULDN'T SAY ANYTHING
because it was my wife's friends, they seemed like her parents'
friends or they were distant relatives in a house, big, a night of
driving and a place to stay was fortunate because we knew we
could, both tired and needed someplace to sleep, it wasn't
arranged but my wife said we might stop and we weren't unexpected. That's how I remember it but it was an area I wasn't
familiar with, vast dark desert or plains and a farm house occasionally and no cars on the road, you don't consider the route
carefully when you're young, just getting there, and something
will turn up like the friends'. A dark house with dim light-bulbs
and wood, floors and the wood outside with the look of weather,
I say weather to describe the wood, walls with faded wallpaper
and warm from a furnace, this must have been in the basement
and the people were dark, somehow, I think the word is reserved,
possibly because of the lateness. This seems to imply blame but
I don't mean that either, after 10 is late to drop in though, you
walk directly into the living room of the people, farmers or they

must have been poor because they were sheep ranchers, the smell
of lanolin said this. My wife and the woman exchanging greetings
like shaking hands or I can't remember, but a hug, me standing in
the background of the room with something in my hand, I
remember it, and the man, a girl is the daughter of a relative or
she lives with them because she was a relative visiting, up this late
means a weekend for the girl or it becomes a habit when people
visit their relatives for the summer. The man, sitting in a chair
with smoke in his mouth from his pipe, it makes me think of my
feet on the carpet, rug is a better word, planted is the word. He
doesn't think of getting out of the chair, seem to, or watch the
women or he doesn't want to do anything, this is why I say dark.
It isn't too late to sit in the living room with the people but the
girl is sent to bed, the girl says something, goodnight, to my wife.
Sitting down on some furniture they had and beer was offered, it
seemed polite so we accepted the beer, I thought I'd get comfortable with the people with a beer in my hand but I was too tired
for a beer, it made me comfortable to hold it but it made it hard
to pay attention as I got tireder, not paying attention, to keep
something going with people who aren't used to others, and I
didn't have that ability either. My wife had something to talk
about with the woman, automatically, their past experiences
together and they didn't have to talk about something else, but
this made it worse, leaving the old man and me to ourselves since
we knew nothing of it we couldn't understand. You listen for
awhile but it's boring and meant something I don't do very well,
come up with something. He was older than I was, I was young,
this is why I called him old, and that left some things out, some
things you might know how to talk about but you don't know if
you should if someone is older because it's natural to talk about
games, for instance but I didn't know much about sports either.
Finally the man began something that I didn't understand but it

was important because it was a conversation, something about
himself rather, a story, what he did in New York before he was
married at a college there where he studied something like business or economics and it was part of a story about his job in his
earlier life, a job is the wrong word, before he was a farmer and
hard times. He mentioned the names of a number of people and
they were names you'd know, like politicians or famous people,
and they were either his teacher or he later worked for these
individuals and this experience made him an executive in the
insurance business, a series of businesses or different companies
that wanted his services, I think, and it gave him a life with the
woman in New York City, his wife and this was when their kids
were being born, it was easy because it was before the Depression.
When the beer came he was still in his chair and sitting back and
his pipe, but by now he was sitting forward the way you will
when you warm to your subject, if that's the right expression, but
it isn't always easy to pay attention to someone when they do if
you have to, if you have to pay close attention if no one else is
around for them, what if they ask a question. But something
made me want to, it wasn't hard to like a man that would tell you
a story about himself and I liked his enthusiasm for something in
the past about his life, a lot was important to him. He went back
to the businessmen in New York City, dark suits, pinstripes and
the word wing-tip brogues. Often there was a merger and he was
part of that and once the threat of bankruptcy but his friends
helped and it wasn't, business lunches were for deals. With his
imagination and his instinct for a deal he was popular in business,
important and his friends encouraged him. And of course, New
York City was the theater and Central Park, they took taxis
everywhere and Fifth Avenue where the wife would stroll. But I
started to realize something was left out or it was going wrong,
missing and I knew I wouldn't find out, because his wife inter-

rupted and the first time it seemed rude, mean might be a better word, there was something strange when she told me not to pay any attention to him, he was crazy, or a word like crazy, I don't remember if it was the first thing she said to me but I was part of it, she meant her husband but it was that violence of getting hit. Soon she said it again like getting hit, hate flashed wanting to hit back, and in the face though but it didn't make sense, if you don't control it, or it's too violent and too intense and making sense of an over-reaction like a punch, just because a woman says something you know the meanness of it did something to you, it's the hate you get. You can't help it, it had an effect. The man seemed to mumble something and I think it did something inside him, it's where he seemed to go, and the story was over after once or twice he must have felt crazy, maybe she said idiot but a word like hitting someone in the stomach and you're watching. My wife saw something was wrong with me I think because she asked and arranged for us to go to bed saying something about a long trip tomorrow and a long time on the road reading maps etc., it made your eyes feel like closing, it was late and it was time. They sent us to the bedroom of one of the children, the woman told us which one and my wife knew where it was upstairs up the old stair case, varnish was worn off the banister from all the years of hands, old house I think I mentioned it would have this wear, and darkness like the dim light in the bedroom from the small bulbs they must have used everywhere to save electricity, but a large bed surprised me, for some reason, and a quilt was on the bed, feathers inside and it had become extremely heavy over the years, I don't know why that happens but it seemed to push us into the mattress from its heaviness. I don't think we said anything that might be about the man and the woman, rather I know my wife didn't explain it though it was probably obvious it was on my mind, I'm not usually that silent, maybe she couldn't.

I had the feeling she knew the answer but it's not hard to imagine, she thought it wouldn't be right to say something then, where we were or at that time although later she never did, that I can remember either. Instead something she did to comfort me at a time like this was common when she knew I was upset, but something was wrong because it usually meant sex, in fact I think it always meant it because of the way it started, her hands on my body would and it always worked and it comforted me, the sex but the other touching. We both were afterwards. On my naked chest to begin with just that much pressure takes out the tension somehow with her soft hands and a few minutes of this gets me relaxed and begins to kiss me on my mouth and kisses my ears. The same thing usually makes me hard by now, and her breasts and their nipples, her hand gently on my balls underneath, but she did and she noticed I didn't get hard, she must have asked about the problem, she said what's wrong. The sheets, I told her, it was the other people's house after all, their children's bed. I must have known we could be careful about the sheets though because we knew how to from other times and other people's beds but it was the man and the woman, I think I was still upset, angry, or something. She kept rubbing my body but she stopped kissing and you could tell she was disappointed, it's understand-able but I guess I was thinking and I thought of the bed and the children and the people had sex to have the children, they lived in New York City. Something made me, I said I love you, to my wife but it didn't sound right, I don't like to say it and I often don't, I should say never but it was the disappointment from the sex.

BEFORE I MET YOU I knew some people, a friend from a year in college introduced me to a jazz musician, a jazz musician can wear dark glasses all the time but it was because he didn't like the way his glass eyes looked, he showed me and I agreed, it was spooky. A jazz musician can and a blind man always wants to but they're both the same, green. He didn't live in a house, he was old, not old but old enough and lived in an apartment where he lived with a wife and her southern accent was just right for making fun of him. She didn't mind it but she always had to take him where he wanted to go and do the shopping, most of it and everything but it meant the musician could have a job when he was young in the musicians' union and they lived like this, he liked her cooking and something said he was glad to have her, insulting each other but it was funny, she said you're blind as a bat. It was an old building of little apartments in an old section of town, not run-down but the building would be torn down some day, and some others in the neighborhood were already, it was too bad because they said they lived there for 25 years, not a nice apartment, with a lot of crabgrass in the yard and needed a paint job and cracks in the plaster but they were used to it, an electric keyboard was in the living room and he knew exactly where it was and he knew where to find each step, and he didn't fall down. He couldn't see it naturally but he liked to listen to the tv, programs and games, he could imagine what it looked like, and it was on all the time the times I was there, especially baseball games, the wife liked it and the man knew where the controls were in front of his chair. Dinner was like food from a different country, and the way she talked like a southerner at their house when I was invited, but it's hard to know what you can say about a person's blindness, ignoring it but it's obvious you'd think about it. He made it easy though because he told a joke about an eyeball highball: glass of water he kept his glass eyes in by the side of the bed at night, or it got loose and rolled across the room and a musician in a band didn't know what to do, it was coming to him but it was about to get away, a joke was made, you could tell they were old jokes but the people laughed and it made me laugh from the feeling of it. The musician told a story about a dream, it seemed like a dream because it involved seeing, it was a huge park in a foreign country with kids everywhere in the playgrounds and they could run behind the water falls of wading pools, adults were parents and there was room for hundreds of teenagers to come to the park together to throw balls and play badmitten in a field below, acres, taking pictures in groups and playing badmitten. People came on trains from all around, for miles. The musician had a job, it was to play music in the loud-speakers when the park closed but he didn't like something about the job because they made him play stupid music with no character, if that was the word, programmed to be the same just to say the park was closing, like chimes. He said it never failed though, as soon as he started playing the music, five o'clock, five-thirty, whatever it was, every single person in the park would stop what they were doing and they all left, the musician would keep playing as the crowds walked slowly up the hill out of the enormous field with their stuff and filed out of the park along the pathways to the exit and even though he was playing stupid music it made him feel a wonderful sense of power. His wife said, oh, Raymond.

the woman
and the cop

▼

1.

TWO THINGS, a house in the mountains when I was a kid: other kids, and a grey day, a kind of party of grownups, from the Union or the family. This is all but it comes back and I expand it, to cousins, a wooden porch with moss from all the wet weather all year around, mountains in the northwest part of the country. A kid wasn't supposed to but he was throwing rocks into a nearby ravine, chucking rocks and it hit someone on the forehead, painful sound of the rock and bone it hit, and there was some blood, wet forehead from blood and it was lightly raining but it was a dirty wound, a rock. Obviously, some parents got involved, and everyone was alright, there was some peroxide, but the kid felt bad from hitting him, everybody did. This kind of wound could happen to my son in a couple years, happen now, in any number of circumstances, could hurt, but you have to go through things.

2.

I'll tell you something about bullies: just hit them in the face once, the time Alan Wynn used to humiliate me on the bus, day after day with his taunting mouth and finally just got off at the bus stop and let him have it, in the face. It scared me but you feel power from it, his mouth bleeding from his braces and sent him home crying. A handful of fist-fights after that, some violence in self-defense in college once when I was attacked on campus by four townies after money. You kiss with braces and they don't seem to mind, as much as you do, self-conscious, but kissing and fucking you, what does it mean to fuck someone and he has braces? Braces are the last thing my parents paid for in my life. It looks like the technology has improved and it doesn't always look as bad now, but my son wants braces. *But wants.*

SOME FRIENDS HAD A LARGE CABIN in the mountains, an old, wooden, almost lodge, and with moss-covered porches, years of accumulated junk under the porches and roofs with gables, shake shingles with life growing on them. It was well-built, and it felt solid when a woman went there with her son, gathering of friends and acquaintances each year and an especially overcast day of late summer, cool, too. But a fire in the fireplace made it pleasant and the company, which she inevitably enjoyed—but by herself this year as a widow—and moving among the clusters of people standing by the fire with jeans and their hands in their jean pockets or people sitting on various old couches and furniture, musty but comfortable, arranged around a number of rooms. Getting involved in conversations and the people would take her differently, but what was different? It was her, she had to admit this was a difference: alone. She said, he'll run the country into the ground, but she said it's the decade and he's simply the right man for the job, but the diction was part of a husband and not her own anymore. The result was restlessness and lingering on the edge of a group of people before moving on to another group, inserting a comment when she could so she could feel part of it.

There was alcohol, and some food, the first thing was to get her son situated and to make sure he got the food he wanted from one of the tables with pot-luck. A glass of red or white wine would come after this. Of course, he was sulking, from having to come when his friends wanted to play at home, but she knew and told him there were other kids at the party, gathering rather, although she knew this would not change his temper until the actual playing with the other kids, overcoming whatever awkwardness. Now it had and it was out of her hands, she was glad for it, to some degree, because she would still have to keep an eye out, but this was more or less a permanent condition of a parent, and there were others, there. The year before a small child wasn't watched closely, child of a "hippie" couple who were friends with several of those there, and got lost, the whole company combing the woods finally found the boy asleep in a ditch at the base of a ridge, cold but asleep, two in the morning. Someone said the obvious, it cast a pall. Something bad like a scrape would happen every year. A husband meant it was her role to be protective of the son, but she let it go and she could concentrate on the other guests. Or she could send her son off to the school bus by himself, like a natural thing, and not have to interrupt her work while he did things of that nature. Other mothers with their young children wait at the curb every day but she simply fights off a feeling of guilt, because the nature of your responsibilities changes. It was hard, but in some ways there were more freedoms after the death of her husband.

Suddenly he died, nothing pointed to it and no one could have said it might happen soon, last year for instance. From his death she questioned what it meant to be a mother and what was superfluous, arranging music lessons and policing the practice of it, but the bills had to be paid and the pressures of money put a new perspective on it. Somehow her son sensed this, taking it over by grooming himself on his own initiative and taking time from playing to practice, these were the most obvious things she could point to. She could have talked about the things that troubled her, doubts, etc., quietly interrupting her husband—it was his study, he's alive and he's sitting at the large slab of wood used for a desk—who puts aside the task at hand, leaning forward in his chair long enough to discuss their son and various dilemmas that would present themselves as he went through the inevitable phases. It was another perspective—not objective, the child's other parent after all—but they agreed their combined attitudes gave "dimension" to an outlook on rearing him. Ultimately she resented that his role was to validate, when she would bring up a position or some aspect of the child-parent relationship that was problematic, like approaching her own father for permission. But it was both of them, she had to admit that. It's a cliché but it really is society. It was still his study in many ways, most, hers now if she could use it but the bookshelves and books that filled them had been used and written in by her husband and the work in filing cabinets that remained unfinished, because his life was too, was unfinished too. He was still in it, because she recognized his authority over the space of it, meaning thought, but she wasn't sure how much her activity as a parent was influenced by what-ever ideas her husband had about it. It pissed her off nonetheless, the possibility of it, and unable to stop thinking about it she went outside standing under the porch roof to check on her son.

She doesn't see him but he couldn't be far with the other kids, and it isn't time to be alarmed—she has a good sense of this—but she wanted to take it this far. There's a man on the porch, familiar from last year. She remembers he lives with his mother, nothing more, but they talk and she finds out he's now a "police officer" in the city. She wasn't going to ask about the mother, but he brings it up, to justify his new career, e.g. the expense of the police acad-emy, but his mother is old now and certain needs are satisfied all around, it's a home for them both and a wholesome environment. Mothers and sons again; of course, her story is different, but she's impressed by this living arrangement—the obligation of a son, and the idea of wholesomeness argues for it—and agrees to take a walk in the woods, the wet green ferns on a path, to a small lake down the way where they might find a row-boat. Thinking about a row-boat irritates her though, because she assumes a man would pick up the oars automatically, and she wouldn't say anything about it. But he doesn't but he simply pushes the flat-bottomed boat off the bank and it drifts into the lake and the oars are next to each other on the bottom of the boat, should she pick them up or is the intention to simply drift? Here she missed her husband, whom she could resent for the possibility of making a decision and his contribution to her passivity, just that he was a man and intimacy made her feel free to direct this resentment at her husband, or she could find ways to express it. With a stranger she couldn't, though it was resentment at a relationship that he represented, too, especially a cop. They drifted, and the cop didn't say a word, just looked all around at the shore of the lake and the water and she can't believe she does but she feels rage at him for a decision not to row the boat.

They drift to the other side and the only conversation is of her husband, I knew your husband, you know. I didn't know that. I was at the funeral. No, I didn't see you. You were in front, and I was in back; but I noticed that some people are lovely, alone in that grief, someone could fall in love with you. This seduces her and sex is a question by the time they get back to the near bank. Of course, it's out of the question because of her son, locating him, she preempts it by saying she has to go back to find him. But something is started and they walk back together, sight the kids and this is enough to reassure her of his well-being, and it's time to rejoin the people inside the cabin.

She joins the group of people assembled around the fireplace, the cop does too, and seems to know something about what they're talking about, from a unique perspective; he says my partner had to shoot someone the other day, guy was swinging an axe at him and what could he do. Naturally, he didn't want to kill the guy, but you don't have a lot of time to decide I'll shoot him in the thigh. They wonder if he carries a gun while off-duty, something tells them a policeman does, they look for a bulge and they wonder why he couldn't shoot him in the thigh. But it's too late to continue their conversation after this, police brutality had been a legitimate topic, but they wanted to keep it abstract, and different topics come up but nothing takes off. It's natural for people like this to mistrust the police and they begin to take opportunities to move away to different groups, only the boring ones remain by the fire. The cop soon moves off, outside again, and this time the woman follows him, they share something and it's that it's awkward for others to talk to them, the closeness they began to feel is intensified by this awareness. She says how did you know my husband, the husband again but the cop doesn't mind, the guy is dead and she doesn't seem to be in any anxiety over a memory that might be in the way, he remembers her willingness of the boat, interrupted only by responsibility as a parent. It turns out there's a long history, back to boys in grade school all the way to graduation when the dead husband went away to college. The cop tells her a number of anecdotes, to illustrate the sequence from walking to first grade together and the gutters they played in until the dead man's behavior at high-school basketball games, fanatic fan, got a technical called against the team once for running down on the court and making threatening gestures at a ref for a bad call, etc. They lost contact after that, little by little, and then he was dead. He said, you met him soon after that, because he knows from letters about the college romance. The cop decides not to ask but he remembers being curious about her, fucking, at that age, consideration for his friend more or less prevented him from asking him at the time, and both were timid. It makes him glad now to have this curiosity and the day ends in this condition of wanting to know more and wanting more, but he knows her skepticism about a man means extra care, it's not lost on him.

He says I wanted to show you something, before you go, and leads her to the woods; there must be a good way to prepare something for the future. She doesn't know what to expect because she doesn't know how to trust a man she just met, but she goes because she wants to see what it is, it's the new her. They go to the woods and he pulls back a parka he has on with one hand, there's the bulge. It's under his shirt, he takes it out and it's got a short barrel, round magazine, the real thing. He does something and turns the magazine around, clicking, and bullets come out into his hand, he hands them to her, the feel of heavy bullets in her hand and the heavy feel of the soft metal of several lethal bullets, has a benign feel. But she thinks of one entering her thigh, at great speed and splintering the bone, and she thinks of a pistol-whipping, although she isn't sure exactly what it is she can use her imagination. He gives her a bullet to keep and she takes it, charmed by this gesture, but on the way home she wonders.

3.

Showing your wife a clipping by a prominent psychologist that says kids should be independent, to argue the point, because you think she's too protective, and sometimes seems obviously an issue of men or women, and kids, the man wants to let go, and vice versa. She has to admit you've got something because she says some of those things herself, but she counters with an article about love, how to keep it or stay in it, something of that nature, and it seems undeniable so you both pin them up on the bookcase. You reverse it and you wonder what happens to them when you fight, your kids, once in the car driving in that proximity with the back seat, where they are, and screaming your hatred, even if your kids are there; incoherent. All those years of it trying to get a purchase.

life is hard
for you

▼

IT COULD BE AN OPEN WINDOW in some town you might see a kitchen table with four chairs around it through the window a man with a baby is walking back and forth, in his arms and his head bent awkwardly to the baby, he must be screaming, the man should read a book to the baby, or it could be about the baby.

HEADED FOR THE WOODS thinking it would calm me down walking on some grassy paths there, with certain birds in the trees making their noises and various mushrooms on the ground, and plants, you spend your life trying to figure out something then something comes along to change it, you find a place like the woods to figure it out: marriage and standing in front of a priest and your love would mean a different kind of world to live in, or the birth of a child, seeing the head pushing and the head comes into view and goes back inside, birth when everything comes squirting out and a baby and another kind of world would mean it again, to try to figure something out (more time anticipating would have answered that, but hindsight always says so). Moving around a lot when the kids were young and these things would happen in life and go right by you, the first jobs and the first

houses made of painted cinder-block and glass blocks to let more
light in but it was always dry desert in West Texas or then the
climate of East Texas. Nothing lasted, and made us irritable, with
little kids "to feed." I'm saying the obvious: living complicates
itself. But it seemed like it was getting worse, walking with my
"infant son" on my back, merest infant strapped on in a contraption designed for that purpose, and no way to get out of how
frustrated it makes you: nothing can. The woods could help but
at a time like that you can't think of anything to a bad situation
with a baby and the situation with his mother made me furious
with him, to use the word "fuck" with a baby—fuck you, when
the baby wouldn't stop crying or demanding.

Or you can say you've heard the silence that comes when someone asks
a question it might cause anger or the anger could make someone feel
like he has to walk out if he shouts from anger there's a small park with
some dead limbs he picks up one of these and smashes it against the
trunk of a tree, he does it again, and again.

HEADED THROUGH THE WOODS and it came out on the third
hole of a public golf course, the rough of it where plenty of trees
still are, high grass, and East Texas is the only place you can see an
armadillo on a golf course here in the rough. Some say Louisiana.
This would calm me down, and it did to see the armadillo,
coming out into the rough from the woods and look out there
and see the golfers, sometimes one you know, but there's a certain
satisfaction because they can't see you. It always helped, sometimes I would sit down if something bothered me that I couldn't
figure out or that happened or something about some people, to
get away from a situation. If the baby was asleep on my back I
could watch different swings of the men and where the balls
went, some of the things that were said by different golfers I

could hear, the obvious stuff very clearly. My baby was sleeping, I would have gone to the place I normally sit on a rock, but a girl was laughing and I kept hearing it, laughing and the first thing I thought was sex. My plan was ruined and made me start swearing again, beginning with more moderate words, eg., goddamit. I kept softly swearing, I started to, it made me remember the situation of my baby's mother, sleeping in bed and facing the opposite direction or I'm facing the edge of the bed and asleep. Two people sleeping in the same bed, two people having sex in the rough of the golf course, what if a duffer hit a ball in the rough. The embarrassment alone said they should have kept out of a public place with their sex, and there are reasons society says so: you shouldn't have to run across it and be reminded of something even if you aren't a golfer. If a man with a baby would show up, this would be awkward enough to make up for my ruined time, though, and an excuse was to upbraid them. But a girl was lying alone on a blanket and I saw her reading a book that made her laugh out loud, if someone was tickling her it would. I looked at her and she would laugh, turn a page, read, laugh. 21, 22 and you could call her plain but the idea of sex and the laughing had put it in my head that she was, I couldn't stop thinking that the laughs meant stimulation. For me suddenly it did and humiliated me from the thoughts of embarrassing them, and the stimulation was a humiliating experience like a wet-dream or an experience like masturbation. Turning to leave and she wouldn't notice me, quietly and I could go home. She did though and said something shy but it was friendly to make me feel welcome, a man with a baby on his back, what was there to worry about in that. Nothing. Obviously I didn't want to but the only thing I could think of was to ask her what book she was reading. It was lucky that at that time I always wore a tie and I took a minute to tighten it, it made people uncomfortable but it meant authority. She felt like she had to answer, standing there in my cowboy boots with my hands in my jean pockets.

———————————

Two people could have a tape player put in the car on trips they could hear music they liked the songs that told long stories about car-hops on roller skates or songs about making movies could make them feel good but the music was a long pause of silence when a question didn't have any answers they were pissed. The sound of snow.

ANOTHER ONE WAS A HITCH-HIKER, and it was me and my wife driving outside a small mountain town in New Mexico where a lot of people from Texas would go for vacations—presumably because of no mountains in Texas—where they liked to ski. Jokes were about Texans buying up New Mexico. Sex was frequent before the kids and in the car and she gave me a blow-job while I was going 60 on the highway, you could see a girl holding a flag or a sign to slow down the traffic sometimes from road construction. One lived in a small trailer, no car, and she had to hitch from there back to her trailer after work on the road each day, thumb was the verb. The blow-job was before we met her, it was a stretch of road like a highway of little attention to the traffic and holding me deep inside with just that much suck to build up sexual tension and save it for the night in bed and making love, like a technique. Later we began seeing the road construction and machinery and always heard girls made good money, standing there and they turn the sign for the traffic to stop, or go slow, depending on the enormous dirt-machine and the approaching traffic. A machine, the back tires as big as your car and with treads, with an operator inside and you don't know what he does in there or what goes in, except the dirt of a mountain, girls get dirt in their pores from standing in it all day, and looked tough with their hair and in tight jeans. She ran to get in and we felt friendly when we stopped because of the sex and our skiing vacation and a hot springs, why not join us for a meal in town where there was a diner, we said, the type of girl that would never pass up a meal if it was a meal on us. This made me wonder about sex and how she managed it, love, and sex. They spoke of their old men and their old ladies, it was part of it of the road construction life. Not much love in it in the construction business, the dirt and machines, having sex and there's dirt in everything, but when we found out she stole our money I had a different idea, if you'd steal it from someone who bought you dinner, and pissed me off but it made me sad. Years before, I wasn't married, I visited a woman and she was married to a construction worker and lived in the mountains building roads over high passes and I went with his friends and him into the woods with a handgun and we shot it at things, cans, stuff that we could hit on the side of a mountain and there was a lot of beer involved and didn't come back to the house until dark. And I had a guitar with me.

———————

He can hear the radial-arm saw and the jointers go on at 7:00 everyday he goes to his bench and his apron is stiff with dried glue where he wipes his hands he ties it on the idea of his kids is the only way to get used to different jobs assembling millwork the foreman brings them stacked on carts with a set of prints he can't get used to the idea of a time clock though.

YOUR SON BECOMES A BOY and you go watch as he plays soccer and see him play, it's muddy soccer on a muddy grass field, grass but the recent rain and how they run on it makes large areas where it turns muddy, vaguely in the middle of the field, and makes you think of going to your cousins' in Texas when you were a kid, football. They must have been too young, where you lived there was nothing organized and made you too young to have the equipment and the organized football they had but in Texas they did. Helmets and pads underneath and matching uniforms, with numbers etc., envy made you feel like crying and sharing a bed with them taught you swear words, or dared you to use swear words. Where your son is playing there's no such equipment, it's just a pick-up game on a regular basis they have, but the field has the same character and makes you nostalgic, your father's brother, James, ran a tire shop in a suburb. It's a good game he has there and you're pleased that you feel pride when he gets a goal, just that you're there with a number of other parents, and it's obvious he's happy with himself and proud in front of you when he comes off after the game and winning, the kids shake hands in a line (they rather slap them these days— "high fives"). You walk off and you're liking each other, it's plain to see. He wants to learn to head the ball when there's an opportunity in a game, he could. Meeting your wife after it and it makes you like her too, feeling good about the day and you're all in it, hard to remember if there was a time you didn't. You don't know what it is, why, rather. Ups and downs but you just blame it on sleep at these times from the new baby but you don't think about it and you all go sit by a small stream, the sort of place you might have a picnic lunch or you have had a picnic together there, in your mind is a picture of it. They both had sex on their minds, at a time like that, but they went home and the kids in bed and they went to sleep because of the layers of feelings and they would have been sleeping by that time if they had been able to sort through it. It made them think of a time when there was only one baby, vacationing in a low-key resort hotel in an old town in the mountains but the hotel brought in a metal crib to the room and they were able to have sex without waking the baby, but they talked it over even then, at some point.

———————

Things take her back sometimes, the formica table in her tiny kitchen where she eats hot meals delivered by a service for old people it doesn't cost much and she likes to eat on her old china still standing at the sink she can do her own dishes after one more cigarette the doorbell rings and her grandson and his young wife come in to visit, so young she thinks of herself that young, and fucking whenever she had a chance, but that ended.

I DECIDED TO VISIT my grandmother's grave. Naturally it wasn't the first time, my grandmother died a long time ago before my kids even were born and I'd go every year on a certain date with my grandfather when he was alive but this stopped when my grandfather died and now it was once in a while, to be alone there as a way to sort through something or to think it through, or it could be getting away from something in my life. This is why it may seem strange that I decided to take my son along, not strange, but it may seem that it would be irrelevant but I had a different idea. You can't go back and don't know who your ancestors are in most cases or you don't know them, but it's important to know they're planted, you have to get that sense to know where you come from or you have to know you come from somewhere and where you might go (the only question is really when) especially someone as close as your great grandmother. I expect my son to tell me some day that the experience made him feel grounded, although he's too young now to have that vocabulary, 4. My wife was against it and I expected it, we often differ on things to do to raise the kids, but it was something I felt strong about and I insisted on it and I'm certain it was the right thing. It wasn't a profound moment standing with my son in front of my grandmother's grave (for one thing it's not a fancy grave and has some weeds around the grave marker and it looks neglected) but it meant something and it made me remember when he was a baby, and I thought of a connection between us, him pushing himself out, and maybe he could benefit later on.

class
consciousness

▼

SEEING THE LOOKS on peoples'
faces, a sneer looking over merchandise as they shop, open-air
market and various merchandise that the people are not used to,
some of it, along with fresh fruits and fresh vegetables and makes
them like to come and see what's new but it makes them sneer, to
think about it and to make a decision. Or you see their faces and
they're deep in thought, perhaps a scowl is a better word, as they
hold up an earthenware mug and look at the colors or how to use
it, that you may have made with your hands and pulled the handle
from wet clay, off the pot, it's what you do, a new cone-6 glaze but
the people can't tell the difference. Of course if you're one of the
people set up to sell the merchandise, a craft or something im-
ported, Guatemalan or quilts from Maine, you smile and you have
things to say like thank you or you try to anticipate by saying, can
I help you and you have to act slavish and it makes you feel
inferior, to sell it because the others won't buy something, they
want you to know your place and they have the right to scowl, like
this is a right, like something that is a right not a privilege. How
much is this, the idea that it's really theirs, a matter of the money

and you have to hand it over, like a privilege is letting them buy it. It's not being polite it really is slavish because they have the money, and you want it, you can't say give me the money, so, there are these strategies, and the politeness, it's capitalism and you are in this position. Pissed off.

WAS BUILDING A CABINET, I had built it it was almost ready to go out it was a built-in with pocket doors for a television and a pull-out for a television and there was a wet-bar, veneer counter-top with a bullnose, and open book shelves that scribed to the walls on both sides. It was out of ash and I was finished except for the crown and some adjustment in the doors, after it took three or four weeks and I was about ready to take it apart to send it to the finisher and it would take four more days to install it. It was a good job on it, because I know what I'm doing after all this time, I should say these years, you have to know how to work from prints and do your own layouts. The cabinet had raised-panel doors—a lot of shaper work and I can set that kind of machine up for almost anything, and not everyone can. Especially with veneers, you have to know how your materials are going to behave, to set the cutters and how to run your piece. You can imagine the people who it was for, though, there was a designer involved and he would come and if there were three dividers above the bar he would want to know why the doors opened this way and not like the lower doors, thank god I had a boss to answer questions like this because that was the way it was drawn but he could think of a better answer to satisfy the designer. The designer walked up and down looking it over, and he would ask questions to my boss occasionally, won't this hit when the doors are open, and my boss would say we, like it had been both of us, and my boss would give him answers he knew he would like, up and down and sure enough, before he left he would smile the littlest smile, look over and say something like, it's nice or very nice. I didn't say anything, I tried to make it obvious. This is something I'm pretty good at and I just keep working and don't look up, clamping up edge-banding, and there's nothing my boss can say, because it's not what I'm hired for, why should I have to *I said it's a story about the material conditions of existence translated into the terms of an official version of reality, the "self-activity" of "real individuals" frustrated by the disparity between an everyday reality and the conventions of representation meant to adequately render that reality. I said ideology is deposited in these conventions; it represents the individual's imaginary relationship to the material conditions of his life by offering an officially endorsed simulation of the world for the meaningful world, making "life itself" inaccessible to the individual. What appears to be an economic system dependent on the division of labor is actually an effect of a much more fundamental division, with other, not-so-obvious effects that are responsible for these social stratifications.* Of course he didn't say anything, to get back, but just gave me a look, as a tactic and nothing was different, it was what I expected. *I said this is Karl Marx, bud—the laborer's dependence on an economic system founded on the division of labor, which initially takes the form of a division between mental and physical labor—the mental labor of simulation meant to adequately represent the actual conditions of physical labor—sets up a division within the life of each individual. Any connection the individual has with the real conditions of his existence is contaminated by the dissemblance of ideology and of representation. Divided against himself, the laborer can only suffer a subservient position with respect to capital.* I had wet glue but I wanted to say something, I said go to the market, what they make or they grow and the people pay the money for it, because they have it it makes you lose a feeling for what your work is or what you may have made because it comes back in money, what you do, and becomes something else of a way of getting by, it's somebody's life or how he spends his life or his time, but it's how they see it or how it might seem, no matter what he does. But if they don't or if I don't work for a boss the others won't buy it or there won't be a system for a living, seems like it's how you have to see it, inside yourself, and makes you sorry to be there, or if the designer shows up to remind you, you're pissy.

THEN ON THE WAY HOME after work, I read these instructions printed on a small door in the back of the streetcar,

> Caution:
> before changing
> fuse—
> put car in
> neutral and
> set handbrake,
> turn off ALL toggle
> switches
> except front door,
> chock wheel with
> switch iron,
> pull pole,
> turn off battery
> switch

and it made me feel better because it made me realize that there was no way the designer could get a feeling for it or what it might mean, in his imagination.

Not
Rich

▼

A FRIEND TOLD THEM to move
and it made sense, logic said they should in a situation like theirs
it might not be natural though, working in the city until their
friend pointed it out, who heard of it and passed it on to the
people. A way to move to a place in the country away from the
reality of the city and the things in their life, but they had no
money, you advertise yourself in other words, what you do have.
This had worked for the friend it was obvious, and he was glad to
show them the wording of an ad as a caretaker, kids and all, a
beautiful place on a creek, old stone house and outbuilding for a
small animal like a goat, cheese was the idea, and bought a wood-
stove for cooking from an auction in the neighborhood that was
ideal and it gave them the hope they needed, their situation was
desperate but it was similar, a life in the city, jobs, but poverty.
The jobs didn't seem to matter, and kids to raise. They would
make the most of it by shopping for produce, a market near their
apartment in a working class area of the city, individuals brought
enough produce for a booth from truck-farms in the nearby
countryside, cheese, etc. A city bus was an interesting place for

people and they could catch it in front of their apartment to the
market and back home, the same bus, they took the kids and they
liked the people at the market, smells seemed to follow them
from their homes outside the city and they liked the idea of
vegetables out of the ground.

The man found a job from another man with a family downstairs who worked at a factory for twenty years and the man told
him to go there and it was a job making minimum wage, it
seemed like minimum wage and it was. The wife was a nurse, or a
therapist was the term in a hospital, giving treatments to patients
and a certain code was called out, she would have to rush there, it
sounds like more but it was the same, and two jobs meant getting
up and the kids, school, and the baby went to a babysitter, it had
to be something in a housing project with other kids, a long day
for a baby. It didn't seem like a good situation and it wasn't, pissed
them off but it wasn't their fault, they knew this and they did
their best to think of the good things, you couldn't think of them
though. One had insurance at work as a benefit, this was a good
thing, because the baby fell on some glass and it was a deep cut in
her knee that would require a cast on her leg for a long time while
it healed but it was cute, she could ride her little baby-bike by
putting her stiff cast up on the handlebars. It was something a
poor kid would do, she wouldn't be around broken glass all the
time. The mother came home from the cast, blood was everywhere but a doctor treated her like a child and made her furious,
it had to be a public hospital.

It didn't take a long time, responses started coming in from
the ad in the paper, some didn't make sense from rich people and
some didn't know what they wanted but they were all rich if they
want a caretaker, and they went to look at some, both kids came
because you didn't want to spring the kids on them. Soon they
got a house, but it was a house on a road, no creek, and they

dreamed of an old solid house of native stones like the friend but they didn't get it because it would take patience, but what if you didn't get a house? It was a house with siding, old tractor in a shed and an outbuilding leaked, something would have to be done like a new roof when they asked the people for money: they could do the labor but there was no money for materials, it would have to wait. Inside was nothing, two rooms, one upstairs one downstairs and you divided it up the best you could, somehow lovely wallpaper could make a difference and the kids would have to be upstairs but a huge room might be fun for two kids. A flue was for a stove and they bought a wood-stove to cook at an auction, another stove would heat the house but it didn't make sense, a stove in the middle of an enormous room would be loaded with great pieces of wood because the whole house might not hold the heat. The friend had a friendly fire going, in a potbelly stove.

Behind the house the owner had a hobby, growing pecan trees, the idea was an orchard but it would take twenty years, different varieties of pecan trees were babies, they looked scrawny and you couldn't tell but they would grow. A little tree is planted in a neighborhood when you're a kid and you come back in 15 years its a big tree, it makes you think about the neighborhood. The owner would come with his wife some weekends to the house-trailer parked up the hill and the trees were for their old age. In their mind was someone to live in the house, because it was there all week, an empty house gets run down and a tractor to pull the bush-hog around the trees when it needed it was an exchange. They said there was a plow for a large garden, it seemed like a good deal to the people and it was a good deal, it wasn't by a creek, etc., but it was a place in the country and it was like a home.

The floor looked like a trapdoor in the closet upstairs but they gave up, they couldn't get it open, and the 6-yr-old boy couldn't get it open but he thought the floor of the closet went somewhere if you could. He asked his father to help, the father couldn't but he would later, when he finished. He believed him, but the father had tried already, and he didn't want to wait, looking for something to do because his father wouldn't help him but the boy couldn't do that either so he found a heavy tool that he could carry, it might be for the tractor, and it would be something to try, if the grownups didn't think so. He dragged it up the stairs and it did, pried it open with the tool and no hinges but you could pull it aside and struggle with it, finally he could put it down and finally it was open. But it was nothing, nothing was there and it wasn't deep when he moved the trapdoor, a foot or less down and he saw some big books, or they looked like books with mold on them or he remembered the word ledgers. It was a disappointment because it didn't go somewhere and he hoped it did, and nothing was in it and he hoped it was. But he saw a cardboard box and the cardboard was moldy, and the box was falling apart, he picked it up and it was baseball cards, the box seemed to fall apart in his hands and they all fell down on the floor of the room and made a mess but he got on his knees and they were old baseball cards of old players he didn't know, it was too bad because he liked baseball cards but he liked the ones he knew. They had black spots on them and a damp place like under the floor does this, and the pictures weren't the same anymore but his parents would know them because they were old, not old but old enough to know the players on old baseball cards. Maybe you could dry them out on the stove. He didn't put anything back because he went downstairs to wait for his father, and looking at the things made them fall apart occasionally but there were a lot.

It seemed simple, you give the old things to the people, they owned the house where the things were, but the man said but who found the things, the people didn't know they were here and the house could have burned down some other time or the people would have gotten old and died. She said finders keepers? It was sarcastic, but old things are worth a lot of money and the owners already had a lot of money. They didn't know what to do and they didn't do anything, but they told the boy not to say anything about the old stuff and he understood, something said not to. He was surprised his parents thought the old books were better than the baseball cards, but a ledger could be valuable to the county or the government because they keep records of old things like titles, or it looked like old deeds, a deed is worth a lot of money and there were a lot. Baseball cards are good but this is where the money is, it's something a kid can't be expected to know. Or auctions, they might get rich, you could say there was a reason they ended up in a house with siding, no creek, and so on. Also living in the city, thinking of it as dues convinced them to, getting rich from the old things and the question was, how? There must be "houses" or agents they could contact and there were but they didn't know where to find them, not in the phone book was obvious. But they said it wouldn't hurt to look, and looking under auctions were some names but they were for old cars and animals unless you went to the city, this was an option but the government came first. An auction might sell the baseball cards but there were surveyor's offices and the court might be interested in the ledgers for their records. They remembered the name Orphans Court from their marriage license, it wasn't the right place for a ledger but someone might know who did. It was a good idea but it made them nervous, what if they accused them of something, or the land the pecan trees were planted on, a deed might mean the people wouldn't have the pleasure of the trees as an orchard, the people were rich but they didn't want to take something away like the orchard. Or the house where they lived now, it wasn't the city. They had to give some more thought to the ledgers, it might be a risk to get money for them or the possibility of not getting anything. But the baseball cards dried out and it was time for the baseball cards. The newspaper said you could get rich from old baseball cards, and seeing something on tv about it. The boy was glad because it seemed like something of his. They might have to forget about the ledgers, they should put them back and close the trapdoor or they could give them to the people after all, who might be pleased, they wouldn't have to say anything about the baseball cards. But they were discouraged, the auctions in the area came first and they expected it, livestock, cars and tractors, but auctioneers and people sitting at the desk and a smile felt like they were laughing at the people, with their two kids and holding baseball cards, it made them wonder about getting rich, if an auctioneer didn't think so. But the auctioneer was only interested in animals and tractors, how could he know about baseball cards? The man went by himself after that but his luck was bad, it was a shame but they didn't have the newspaper with the article telling how to get rich, it was a long time ago and there was no point thinking about it it seemed like it was time to try the city.

The man was driving the old truck they had, the baseball cards were on his mind and the same question, what to do with the baseball cards or should they give more thought to the ledgers? On the road a hitchhiker had one thumb in the air, it was a county road with a number and the hitchhiker was obviously on his way somewhere, the man was a hitchhiker before his kids so he stopped the truck off the road. The hitchhiker ran up to the truck and it was the usual thing, throwing his duffel bag in the bed of the truck, sometimes they have guitars, you didn't want to make someone wait when they did you a favor. He mentioned where he was going but it was far and it was late, and something gave the man an idea, he invited the hitchhiker over until the next day. He said he would, he could sleep in the man's warm house and not in a ditch by the road, or he might stand by the road all night and he might get an all night ride to a city, but it was settled.

The wife was pleased to have the hitchhiker for dinner, she was a hitchhiker too and those memories by the side of the road and the kids were pleased with his friendliness when he talked about the road. One story was about a truck and eight hitchhikers were packed in the bed of the truck, in the back, but it was cold so it was good, because their bodies helped. They wanted him to and it was decided the hitchhiker would sleep upstairs on the floor, everyone was satisfied with the arrangement and they went to bed. They didn't go to sleep though because the boy wanted to show him the baseball cards, he thought the hitchhiker might be old enough and might like them, who they were and it would impress him. The hitchhiker said he did, he was a baseball card collector, not a collector but he appreciated baseball cards and knew something about them and had baseball cards when he was a kid and had some knowledge of them, he was amazed by the old baseball cards. The boy told the story of the trapdoor and the tool, and they stayed awake for more than an hour turning them over and the hitchhiker told him what the numbers on the back mean, arranging them in teams made the boy happy.

In the morning the boy wakes up, it's odd, he looks around first but the hitchhiker's not there and goes downstairs, nobody down there is up and he's gone, so are the baseball cards, it was a thief. They couldn't believe a hitchhiker was a thief, a myth about the road told them not to but they figured it out, it meant being on the road and the others on the road. They were pissed, because naturally they weren't on the road but he slept in their house, and weren't they part of it? But it made them too sad to do something, they could chase after him but it made them too depressed. It was the city all over again, to have your things stolen and this bad luck, first the ledgers now the baseball cards, it might be a lesson about things and getting rich from them but the worst thing was the boy's disappointment, they couldn't tell but they knew he didn't like old baseball cards. It was the hitchhiker though, and showing the baseball cards to the hitchhiker, and what would the boy think about his parents and their past as hitchhikers, did it mean they were thieves?

It was time to hook the bush-hog up to the tractor, the grass was getting high around the pecan trees and it was time to forget about getting rich, hitchhiker, etc. The man asked his son if he wanted to ride on the tractor with him, the controls and the feeling of a farmer and the steering wheel, or pretending it's heavy machinery, you get the feeling of a machine. The boy was surprised he would but his father asked and right away he said he did, it was the first time his father asked him to ride the tractor and the boy wanted him to, he didn't think he was old enough. But if he was he was proud of himself to ride it with his father. His father was thinking, he said there's enough land, we should plow some land for a truck-farm and take it to the market in the city, and made the boy think of himself as a kid at the market. His sister was in the garden and he knew his mother was watching from the nearby garden, he wanted to wave to her but he tried not to look at her, to feel like it was natural to ride a tractor. In a week they got a letter in the mail, it had their names on it and it was addressed to them. They opened it and it worked out, because they didn't know what happened but they thought they did, it didn't say where it came from. Inside were two hundred-dollar bills. But a feeling of bad luck was already gone, they didn't need it anymore because it seemed like the luck was moving out of the city, but it made them feel better, they weren't rich but they could get the leaky roof fixed at their expense, maybe they could store seeds there.

watching
movies

▼

T HEY WERE IN A BAR and were
waiting to go home with somebody, hoping to, it was somewhere
in the East and the bar, and a number of bartenders to give out
drinks of various sorts, with ice, or beer and the people at the bar
would look at them and when others came in, they would look at
them. One had taken care to dress himself and bathe and shave
and he looked his best. They both did, but he preferred to sit and
talk but his friend liked to dance and went to the dance floor for
disco music with someone, his friend gone and he didn't know
what to do with himself, without a friend and he didn't want to
get involved in anything, at the bar, because sometimes someone
would come over and he might go home with him, if he liked
him, there was a better chance. But he didn't have much to put
into it, for some reason, and decided to stay for the rest of his
drink and it was pleasant, to watch the action, loud music, to pick
out a word or a phrase from the din but you didn't want to do it
for longer than that. It was something he always came to, it
seemed like, and he'd go, a rainy night, light rain, and decide
what to do or to watch on tv or he had occasionally gone alone to

a movie. One was about a Hungarian woman in the United States, black-and-white and it was a new, young director, his third film only and he liked them, something about them how they resolved formal problems. He enjoyed seeing a film by himself: still, he wanted the companionship and sleeping with someone, sex, picturing warm skin, the pressures soft and hard as you find different ways of touching, perhaps, massaging his prostrate with one finger and how hard you both get, and perhaps coffee in the morning. The Hungarian woman had come to stay with her aunt in a Midwestern city, the look of the Midwest, and the cousin visited her in a little diner, where she worked, from New York and saw this in the bathroom while he was waiting for her to get off:

> if you are cold I'll
> bring you heat like
> I brought the whole
> world my funkey beef

Of course the cousin thought it was dumb, or he ignored it but it seemed like the best part of the movie, vaguely in the background of the shot, not as a message but it showed some imagination. This was in a movie theater where there were few people, art cinema, with two rows and you felt intimate, he wanted to ask a neighbor what he thought of it but you couldn't have a discussion during the film.

Or as a kid, going outside at the drive-in movie, with your parents in a car, and you get out at intermission, go to the concession and there's a bathroom, big men standing in front of urinals and of metal mirrors, with combs in their hands or smoking, you have to be careful the smoke doesn't go in your nose or your eyes when you hold it in your mouth, both hands on your penis at the urinal, to keep the elastic away, the curling smoke and many of them are squinting. The boy looked at the man's penis beside

him, brown, held in the man's familiar fingers, up at his face and
the man looking down, at his penis and peeing. He had a cigarette in his mouth but he knew what he was doing and it didn't
make him squint. A summer night, of stars back outside, and
there are picnic tables in an area closed in by a cinder-block wall,
around the concession building, speakers, if you wanted to sit out
there. He wondered why, always, nobody ever there, and weeds in
the gravel where no cars could go and around the legs of the
picnic tables, and weeds around the bases of each speaker pole,
shared by two cars. It would be a good thing to go to a drive-in
now, with some man, that he was fond of, why didn't he think of
it. There were no drive-ins any more, but he didn't understand
why, not the shopping malls, where a drive-in should be: then,
what. Any drive-ins that might survive are sure to be out West,
thinking they are surely beyond the boundary of the city, cities,
suburbs, and this is where they should go, it would be a weekend
trip into the country, farm land and this is where you see the
giant screen lit up as you drive across country at night, on the
outskirts of a town. It would be a matter of stopping, it doesn't
matter what's playing, spaghetti western, it's the experience of
eating fried chicken in the car with a speaker hanging on the
window and how absurd to have sex in the car like high-schoolers,
the middle of Kansas and your hands on each others' stiff cocks
and the sharpness of your beards. But he didn't and he didn't go
to a movie, but he went to another bar and this time for a few
beers. Everyone was standing around with a beer in their hands
and watching those playing pool walking around the table to the
cue ball with a stick and a cigarette in one hand but it was so
crowded that you felt the bodies and you felt it when people's legs
would brush you. He liked it and he liked so many men in jeans,
the smells, a certain chemistry. It was good, and there was another
area and you could sit up on a ledge and he knew people that

came here and one might come along to stop and talk, it was what a number of people were doing and some had other intentions and some didn't. But he left without talking to anyone, it wasn't working out. It made him wish he was with someone though, to be outside because there had been a tv movie about the homeless made in the neighborhood of the bar, a man was walking to the train station when a street-person approached him for money and he didn't look at the guy, eye contact, there were always one or two inside the entrance to the train station and you looked straight ahead. It was getting pretty bad, the street-person took a whack at him, as someone put it, it wasn't safe, it was the feeling of the fabric of it all falling apart, society. What's to stop them. Nothing. But walking on, by the nighttime of a demolished neighborhood, for a convention center, rubble, onto the subway, feeling, anyway, he'd be at home soon, and you knew you wouldn't be down there long you just hope for the best for that amount of time. He figures he'd just give them his wallet, no questions, what are they going to do, throw him in front of a train. No. Nevertheless there are some young toughs on the car he steps into and it makes him nervous and gets off a stop early but it was dumb because now he has to walk through a not great neighborhood again, where people are on the street, but you don't look at anyone this late and it's not so bad, he walks through it from time to time. It doesn't matter, it's a not great neighborhood where he lives and goes in and turns on the light and opens a can of beer, it's too bad about tonight but it doesn't matter, e.g., he goes home with someone from a bar, the guy is really drunk and pawing him on the way to the car, and he has to drive because the guy is too drunk and the guy hands him ten dollars to hold, or for gas, it isn't clear. He feels uncomfortable with him but he's with the guy and you can't change your mind now to get out of it. When he's sober, it might not be so bad. But they get to the guy's apartment and his roommates are up and some other people, even though it's late, already morning, but they're show types, with loud show-tunes blaring on the cheap stereo and some of them have dates and the guy he's with keeps pulling him down on his lap or roughly pinching him, there's lots of laughter and more drinking and finally he has to simply make a weak excuse and gets up to leave, it's all he can take. The guy gets mad, really put out and accuses him of some things that don't make sense, abusive, but he can't help it and gets his coat, just leaves in his car and drives off, and feels a tremendous relief from it from being alone. He's pissed, where was the tenderness. But he's gone a mile and remembers the ten dollars, and it makes him anxious because he's still a part of it and immediately turns around and brings it back, knocks on the front door, the guy appears, others looking out behind him to see what it is, and he hands it back with a murmured excuse but it infuriates the guy, who interprets it somehow and refuses to take the ten dollars back, closes the door with some rude words and he gets back in his car and buys some gas with it. The thought of it would make him depressed, a situation of strangers, him in it it would make him want to call his friend, who had likely gone home with the person he went to the dance floor with, but he wanted to call someone, another friend. It was late but not extremely late, he decided to call someone anyway, it was a woman and she answered and said why not come over, the kids are in bed and we could get a movie if you're up for that. It was the perfect solution to have her companionship, and he didn't hesitate but went over there, stopping at a store for a movie. They settled in on the friend's couch and started up the movie, sex was a question, as they drank a brandy and the movie came on. It wouldn't have been the first time, it was simply softer in some ways and uncomplicated in the usual manner with the tenderness they felt it was a pleasure to have sex at times, mouth-jobs usually, a release but there was a lack, for him the hardness of a man, they turned to the movie. In one scene a man is charmed by his three-year-old's dissemblance, when the boy secretly takes a dollar on the bus, from his football-helmet bank, he was playing with it on the floor before they left and the father said what's in your pocket, on the bus when he saw the boy keep looking down there, at his hand in his pocket, he's not supposed to play with money. It was the first time he had thus dissembled, as far as the father knew and the implication was he thought it was cute because it meant independence. Of course it does but it leads to other things and you shouldn't indulge it, everyone knows this, a teenager could turn into a criminal. He pointed this out to her later, in bed as he related the story of the young toughs on the subway.

agonistics

▼

Every utterance should be thought of as a move in a game. To speak is to fight, in the sense of playing, and speech acts fall within the domain of a general agonistics.

—LYOTARD

WALKING OUT INTO THE SHOP, the various half-built units of cabinetry or of furniture and the machinery going, here and there, different saws or planers, etc. and the men at work on it. Approached the bench of one of them, hand-plane on its side and a chisel, handscrews, and asked a question about the progress of the job, out of walnut or the dimensions of the layout, or he makes a comment about how he would do it or how he does it and the guy thinks, you son-of-a-bitch you never even pick one up, he has eyes. But just says my rip-blade is at the sharpener's. He goes over the job with the boss, some changes that have been made because of the architect, and how he has to do some things over because of it, talk about "efficiency." Or if they'd fix the jointer so you didn't have to check it for square every time you run a board. It all came up when the boss decided to start giving out the hours estimated for individual jobs, "so you can have a better idea how we're estimating, and how long things should take." It's not his job, why should he have to, the type of individual who wants to do his work because he knows that vocabulary, of set-ups and joinery, the ways of keeping hand-tools sharp and prefers a water-stone, an isolated world and he has the authority to move in it and a pleasure, because he knows the language, but not that other language of profits and how to deal with a "client." He likes it that way or he wouldn't work for a boss, goes home and he's pissed. His wife says, it's to test your performance. She says don't worry about it, just do your work. His wife says don't forget your father was a union president. When his father was president of the union when he was a kid, khakis and you were a worker. And going to the union hall for a meeting, he remembered going to one and there were men there who worked with his father and one man he knew, was deaf, had taught him a little sign, spelling with the alphabet, and another deaf man was there and they would sign and the boy was amazed, how fast it was. The only thing he didn't like was the grunting noises they made, trying to speak. They all sat down on metal folding chairs in rows and it was nothing he would understand and it didn't seem important except they would shout sometimes, but it was boring. But it made some of them mad and his father had to stay and talk to them, with some other men from the table at the front, it seemed like a bad argument but it was for collective bargaining and you couldn't do it yourself. It meant wearing a tie and he had to go to the airport with a suitcase, call home from his hotel, and brought them little things when he got back. Or looking for bargains during a strike, his father coming home and he had found a bargain on some cough syrup but it doesn't make sense, you try to imagine your father out looking for bargains all day to make up for the money. It makes it easier because his father was picketing, some of that time, but he doesn't find that out until after the strike when his grandfather mentions it, who doesn't like the union and the father is in it, has nasty things to say about the father and makes the boy mad, but what can he say. He doesn't want to get punished. The grandfather says its a union shop so he didn't have any choice, says I bet I can tell you how your father voted on right-to-work though. His grandfather says but he didn't have to become president of those assholes. He says they're not assholes but the grandfather says don't use that language with me.

YOUR WIFE goes to the store and saves ten dollars on coupons: an hour's wages, after taxes.

OR SOME PEOPLE live in the city, car insurance is double and you have to have insurance on your apartment. They "red-line" certain areas but it's not legal and you might have to get your landlord to fix the sidewalk where some roots are pushing it up and cracking it. But they can threaten you and you have to keep asking to have it done, you don't want to lose your insurance. It could happen to anyone. Or take the gas company. They can simply continue sending you bills, you move out and they keep sending them, call and they keep sending them. You ask to speak to the supervisor and you can't believe it, they can't take it out of your name unless you let them in to read the meter. It's not your house but that's all there is to it, it's the gas company and nothing you can do.

Two people were new in the city and they didn't know where to live, asked around and got various answers from different people who didn't understand the question, and finally decided on an area because of the man's job, which he had from where he used to work. They could afford it but it was an eye-opener because he made more money but they spent it all on the city, this business about insurance, also the rent and higher prices, the deductible when their apartment was broken into. They knew it would be more but it was the same, but they said at least there's the city and they took a walk in their neighborhood downtown and it would energize them, to be in the action of it and to see the different sights, of an old city, and the woman's studio, other artists and a new artist at the studio, from another town, was nice but there was a meeting and she would refuse to go by a consensus because she said it wasn't art, a meeting wasn't art, if you had to have one she wouldn't show up. Of course, it isn't, but she said she was an artist and the implication that she didn't have these responsibilities, if she wanted to it didn't matter, she could draw or walking around was art. They couldn't believe it, reasoning with her or arguing sometimes but she would scream at them in different contexts and finally had to leave. Not that they didn't try, but it was all of them, you can't run a studio like that but they learned something from it.

And the man and the woman learned something about city life: the man said it costs too much to work in a studio and said I have the responsibility of the money. She said you can't put money on it, to measure my time, or my life but it reminded her of the obnoxious woman and she said do you think I don't know you're supporting me. He said is that what you want, and she said you know it isn't. It was the pressure of the city and the woman couldn't take a walk by herself, at night, and the man told her not to make eye contact with anyone, they were learning to be careful. A lawyer told them they would win, their landlord wouldn't give back the deposit because of a leak he had to fix, by tearing down a wall, old pipes that leaked on their rug but he could easily appeal and they would still win but it would cost too much. They shouldn't have paid the rent during that time of inconvenience and the cost of the rug but it was too late. It made them mad and they would watch their friends who had grown up in the city and instinct told these people how to be careful, it wasn't something to think about. You don't pay the rent. But they didn't know how to do it and the man couldn't find an amiable way to tell his boss to fuck off, with a joke. His boss was "complaining" to someone who stopped by about the size of the payroll and how it would prevent them from ever showing a profit, etc., it was a joke but it was part of the same thing of harassment. A co-worker spoke right up, said, well you and Byron must be paying yourselves too much then, because we're sure as hell not seeing any of it, and everybody laughed.

To Whom It May Concern:

Enclosed is a carbon copy of a letter I recently addressed to Public Service Company concerning statements on an account that they continue to send me despite my repeatedly informing them that I vacated the premises on October 31, 1989. Apparently, they are having difficulty gaining entrance to the property to read their meter (note that the entire balance of the statement is the result of "estimated" amounts). No action on your part seems warranted at this time, but I wanted to bring this matter to your attention, as PSC seems to be having some difficulty in resolving it. Thank you.

physical therapy

▼

THEY WERE PARANOID about someone breaking in, and it happened a lot in their neighborhood. It was something they had talked about and they both felt bad about it, they wanted to buy a gun, and he knew she was just trying to play the other side of it, she said are you going to sleep with it under your pillow? But it seemed like a good idea, to just buy it, it would stop being an issue, he said I'm going to buy a gun. He said there's a pistol range in the same block, I'll go there after my therapy and learn to shoot it, it's next door. Some friends who owned a handgun had accidentally shot it through the floor of their apartment recently, he was glad she didn't bring that up. It was because she wasn't sure, whether she wanted a gun in the apartment or not. It was a conversation they had often, the pros and cons. But she said, are you going to shoot somebody? He said no. When he left the house she kissed him, casually, on the mouth, but it made him feel like it was a decision and he made sure to take the check-book, where he saw a therapist once a week.

There was a small office, with cardboard boxes stacked in the waiting area, full of patient files, probably the people lived in different states by this time, they had that look of old boxes, they must have. There were some magazines on top of the boxes, in case you had to wait and there was room for one chair, and sometimes he would see someone sitting in it but he never had to wait. The receptionist had a small clock-radio that got a tv station, she'd had a soap opera on when she got his information the first time when she took everything down. Then she took him back and she told them he was an English teacher and this made the assistant say well lets put him to work on that crossword puzzle, where they used to do a crossword puzzle when it came out in the paper, twice a week. He didn't know whether there really was a crossword puzzle until later, or if it was just a joke. It was a joke, but he didn't know if there really was a crossword puzzle. He was able to smile at this but he was too embarrassed to say anything, when people would make a remark like this, in public or at a party. It was the assistant's way of being nice and the man knew this, he seemed like that type of a person, like a construction worker, not a construction worker but like a skilled laborer like a machinist, to make this kind of joke, this and when he told the man to go in the treatment room and take off his shirt, the implication that the therapist would be in there any minute. John will be right with you, the assistant said, and said you can have a seat, pointed at the treatment table covered with white paper, that they replace after each patient from a big roll at the head of the table. It gets wrinkled where you lay on it. It was a treatment room with no doors, to close.

John was there presently and had asked the man the usual questions, about his pain and he pressed in certain spots along the man's spine and asked the man to press against his hand, etc., and asked if it hurt. Sometimes it did, but it always hurt, where it felt like the vertebrae of his neck would grind together and it got into the muscles of his neck and he thought there were some nerves involved. At first the man had the feeling the therapist didn't understand anything about the pain really because of the places he pressed and how he pressed and the things he wanted to know about. He always figured a doctor or somebody knew more than he did, though, so he didn't say anything, but he hoped the therapist knew what he was doing and did something that would help. He was considering acupuncture, since nothing else seemed to work. He was glad when the therapist suggested a routine of traction, for ten minutes each visit, he thought it might pull the vertebrae apart and it might make a difference. First, it was the assistant's job each time to get out the hot-packs and get the man started on them, and he would ask the man questions about what he was teaching or what he taught that day when he did this, and the man would try to think of clever things to say about his students and his teaching, he knew the assistant appreciated irony.

He didn't want to say anything to the assistant about the gun though, but when John came in to hook up the traction device he wanted to say something to him. He knew he would have an opportunity because when the therapist came to hook up the machine he always asked the man something about himself, and when he did the man said I'm thinking of going next door and buying a gun when I finish here today. That so, said John, harnessing his neck into the contraption. I guess it would make a lot of people feel safer, but I'd be afraid I'd shoot myself in the foot. John could say this of course because he lived in the suburbs. He told the man he should take the assistant with him to buy a gun. You're the last patient today, he said, and he knows a lot about them, he has one. The man didn't know what to say to this, but then the assistant came in to get something and the therapist told him the man was going to buy a gun, why don't you go next door with him and give him some pointers. The assistant said sure, I've got some time before my train.

He'd just have to make the best of the situation.

You've got to have a gun in the city, said the assistant, on the way out the door to go to the gun shop. Yes, said the man, that's what I figure. He wanted to seem casual, about it.

When they got in there he was actually pretty glad the assistant had come, he had no idea what kind of gun to even ask for or to look at. He asked the assistant, what have you got. He said a .357 Magnum. You don't need that much to stop somebody, but its a lot more fun to shoot it, you get the satisfaction of the recoil, it's the feeling of that explosion in the chamber, you really get the feeling of how much power that baby has, to go off in there like that. The man said, yeah. Because it made him warm up to the assistant, he seemed to be genuinely helpful, like you would be to a friend and the man was touched. He had only thought to get a small gun, that could wound you. But he was intrigued by what the assistant was telling him, but he didn't want to buy a big gun.

But the assistant said, but look, they have a shooting range, why don't we go over there and they'll probably let you try one out if you say you're thinking of buying one. It was like buying a car, the man thought, but he didn't think the assistant would appreciate this irony.

The assistant was right, the recoil when he shot the gun. It was hard to imagine something could have that much power, he tried to imagine how deep into a tree-trunk the bullet would go, if it would go all the way through, or how big the tree would have to be if it could. They were in the pistol range and there were targets at the other end shaped like men, he was holding the gun out aiming at one but he couldn't hold the gun up, out there at arm's length, it was that heavy and it made the pain in his neck more acute. But he had learned to live with the pain, it was always there, and he held the gun up long enough to shoot one and then he had to drop it down to his side to rest his arm and relieve the pain. He was surprised by the violence of the recoil and the sound, it was enough to hurt his eardrums, the shock of an explosion. The gun salesman said hold it with two hands, here, and he took the gun to show the man what he meant. It was a lot better and he could appreciate the power of it better since he didn't have to worry about dropping it from the recoil. It was the most powerful thing he had ever held.

He shot it several times, until he thought the gun salesman was about to say something about it, it jerked his hands back each time, then he handed it back to him and they went back in the store, his ears were ringing from the tremendous noise of it. The salesman said do you want to see something smaller, but the man said no, that's alright, and he went home without buying a gun but he thought about it and it made him think about carrying a gun and feeling it under your coat, hanging in a holster.

The man's wife said she was just as glad he had decided not to buy a gun when he got home and she asked about it. He said I shot it though, you wouldn't believe how much power something like that has. She said but you weren't thinking of buying a big gun. No, but I wanted to see what it was like to shoot one. I'm just as glad you changed your mind. I am too, he said.

They didn't talk about it any more and the next week he went back to his physical therapy. It was the assistant's job to set up the usual hot-packs and the way the ultra-sound heated so deep you couldn't feel it, all the way to the bone, where there are no nerve-endings. He could fall asleep lying on the paper on the table, on the hot-packs, they were so hot and he would close his eyes for ten minutes, but there was a vacuum cleaner going, he noticed this each time he came and he could never get to sleep because it would get louder and softer as it came closer to where he was

lying. He would just about, but there was always a radio that he
could hear, playing an all-news station and he could catch up on
the news that they played when he could hear it over the vacuum.
And the hot-packs did relieve the pain, while he was lying on
them, and the ultra-sound too, smearing the metal head that
broadcasts the sound-waves around in the cream on his shoulders.
The assistant was doing this before John came in to hook up the
traction and he said to the man, hey, you want to go over and
shoot that gun again. The man acted surprised but he wasn't, he
had to admit it to himself, and he said alright, and they went
back to the gun store to shoot the gun again after his traction and
after the exercises they had him do. He had some time to think
about it lying in the traction, pulling his neck for 15 seconds then
letting up for 15 seconds and he decided he'd buy it.

The man went and bought the gun and they went to shoot it
again in the pistol range, it was a different feeling now that it was
his gun. Because the salesman wasn't out there with them now
and he held it out with both arms extended with his finger
through the trigger-guard, it was like he remembered, the power
of it exploding in the chamber like a little bomb in there, that
threw his arms back and the bullet goes through the target
immediately. There was something special about it.

At first his wife was pissed that he bought the gun, she said it
bothered her, to have it in the house and she didn't see why he
had to buy such a big gun. But they kept it in a drawer in their
bedroom upstairs and a box of bullets across the room in another
drawer hidden under some socks. The idea was that if they heard
someone downstairs at night they could get up and put a bullet in
the gun and shoot it through the ceiling or something. The man
said shoot it through a window, it's easier to fix. But you didn't
want to have the bullets with the gun, to prevent an accident or if
someone came in when they weren't home, the crook would have

a gun. It did make them feel more secure, they both admitted it. But the wife began to complain that she didn't know how to shoot it, in case she was alone in the house, so they went to the pistol range together, the man said that's easily solved. The man showed her how to hold the gun with both hands and squeeze the trigger until she heard the explosion, and she couldn't believe it either, she had to close her eyes when she pulled the trigger and she was afraid she'd drop it. She couldn't hit anything but she shot it a number of times, she said she had to agree with the man, the power of it was incredible, she couldn't imagine it.

They took it home and put it in the drawer in the bedroom and it made them think about it and think about someone downstairs, what they'd do, it made them think they should practice. It seemed like a good idea, not to actually shoot the gun off, but they wondered how long it would take, to get out of bed in the dark and get a bullet and put it in the gun, across the room. Why don't we time it, the wife said, and they decided to set it up. They turned off the lights and got in bed, like they ordinarily would, and the woman had a tiny light inside her wrist-watch to time it when he got up. She said okay, let's say we hear somebody: now, and he got up and went over to the dresser that had the bullets. He was being quiet, taking his time enough so that he didn't make a lot of noise. He got a bullet and carried it over to the other dresser, and opened the drawer with the gun and lifted it out and felt the heavy gun in the dark, feeling for the pin that released the cylinder. He slid the rounded end of the bullet in a chamber in the cylinder and snapped it closed but he realized he didn't know which way the cylinder rotated or which chamber would fire next. He didn't know what he could do, he couldn't fire it off to see if he had the right chamber, he said I guess we have to call this an aborted attempt, and said why don't you turn on the light so I can see if it's in the right chamber. His wife turned on the lamp on the bedside table but she said, but it really doesn't matter if it's in the right chamber, because you can't turn on the light to look if a crook is downstairs. True, said the man but he wanted to check anyway, because he said he was curious.

They talked about it for a minute and they decided they'd have to load the entire gun, all six chambers, it seemed like an easy solution, and they agreed to have another trial immediately. The man got out of bed and the woman pushed the button on her watch that turned on the little light inside and he opened the drawer with the bullets and counted out six, in the dark. But he said it would be faster if I just took a handful, wouldn't it, and he came back to the bed to start the trial over. This time he just grabbed a handful and took them over to the dresser where the gun was. He felt for the gun in its drawer and got it out and started putting in the bullets, one at a time until he had all six chambers loaded and he snapped the cylinder closed. He said it's finished, and his wife called out the time, two minutes, twenty-eight seconds. But the man realized he didn't know if the safety was on, on the gun, he couldn't tell in the dark and he panicked all of a sudden, to be holding a loaded gun in his bedroom, with bullets in all six chambers, it felt extremely heavy. He didn't want to feel around for the safety for fear of setting the gun off, by accident or loosing his grip on it and dropping it and it would go off when it hit the floor, he felt like he was holding a live grenade, the term was live-ammo. Even if he could locate the little lever he wouldn't know which way to push it, he might be taking the safety off. He told his wife, turn on the light. Of course she didn't know what the matter was but she thought she heard something like panic in his voice and she turned the light on and looked over at him, the man didn't know what to do with the extra bullets because he needed his hand free so he could get the gun unloaded, he just opened his hand and dropped them and they rolled around on the wooden floor while he found the pin and pulled out on it to swing the cylinder open and turned the cylinder, emptying the rest of the bullets, from the gun, on the floor with the others. His wife said what was that all about.

The assistant said how's that .357 magnum, he was getting out the hot-packs with long metal tongs. The man was unbuttoning his shirt, he said, fine. He said, we keep it in a drawer. Ever get out to shoot it any more, said the assistant. The man was busy hanging the shirt on a hook, we haven't had to shoot anybody, with it, he said. The assistant said count your blessings. John was walking in and heard and he said, shot yourself in the foot with it yet? The man smiled, but then he lay back, on the hot-packs and closed his eyes, to relax, he said I think my neck's getting worse. It's this damn weather said the assistant.

a problem
of hostility

▼

ANY NUMBER OF THINGS you
could think of, woman on the bus says move your butt over, buddy, to
sit down. You move over and you don't say a word, not all the way over
to make it uncomfortable for her but you don't say find another seat
you old bag, you don't say why don't you learn some manners, or you
don't say what's your problem, to another guy on the bus, when he says
something rude from stepping on his foot, but you don't understand
this until later. Pardon? He says keep on moving and you do and you
just sit down. What's your problem, buddy, you should say find another
seat you old bag. This happens to you, or you should say you do it.
Because it never occurs to you until after something that you didn't
have to just take it, like you're afraid of losing your driver's license. It
would take more than that and you lose something else, self-respect
and it makes you mad inside.

THE LOCAL ELEMENTARY SCHOOL in the evening, the first of the
year where his son goes to first grade, sitting in the room with
the teacher, later, but it begins with everyone in the auditorium
together in chairs, and they have to stand up to say the pledge
of allegiance: the principal: first we'll rise and say the pledge of
allegiance. A shock went through him, to hear this unexpected
thing, and didn't know what he should do, a glance to his wife.
For instance, he doesn't bow his head at relatives' for grace

because he doesn't believe in god. It makes him mad because of what the assumption is, that they would all feel this allegiance that it's a natural thing. He remembers the anger of the bus and it makes him want to remain sitting to do something but it's his son's school and what would it mean to a little boy if they saw his father doing this, he stands up to say it but he doesn't say it.

The teacher keeps talking about the work-books and what they do during the day and he tries to keep an open mind but the classroom is hot, with low tables for children and sitting on low chairs, and the room confines him, and imagines his son would be, too. It makes him critical but it makes him feel mean about it because of the experience in the auditorium that they expect his son to believe it's natural to pledge allegiance. The real fear enrages him and it's that he will. But it's like the bus, he can't say anything or he doesn't know how to say it because of a problem of hostility, he's trying to learn to control his feelings. He does when they're milling about when the teacher finishes her thing he manages to talk to other parents from time to time, who in fact believe in something natural about loving a flag, etc., and manages a pleasant exchange or two but it makes him a hypocrite, he sticks to his wife, he looks through his son's workbooks. They have a baby and he makes an excuse to take the baby out in the hall and walks around and holds the baby until his wife comes out she wants to stay for the library but he says let's go, the baby is fussy. They get in the car and the wife is pissed they couldn't and he's pissed, if someone would understand (e.g., a salesgirl behind the counter—he drops his wallet on the counter—says friendly, flip that thing back here. He manages something like a weak smile or a "polite" smile, until he's out on the street he should have said: you'd be pretty disappointed, or something friendly). He drives and he doesn't say anything about the school and he makes small talk to the babysitter when he drives her home.

The difficulty of time, his time, to do or he wants to take, he wants to leave something. A limited amount but why would someone yell at you, and it's to accomplish. The example of another generation, before, and after. You make a choice.

H E TAKES HER HOME and his mother lives in the same neighborhood, and decides to stop by, as the saying goes and goes in and his mother is there watching tv and smoking. He doesn't like the way it smells and tells her to stop, his mother says I know I should. Two of her husbands are dead, but she puts a good face on it and does a number of things in the community, collecting canned food and she goes to church to find out what she can do on the bulletin board and she believes in God. But she refuses to stop smoking. But his mother welcomes him, she does it with a word and a smile and puts out her cigarette and says for him to come and sit, urges it. She turns off the tv without a regret, the pleasure it gives her to see him, it's the middle of a show. She can see he's glum and this makes it better, because she can do something like comfort him or something like advice. She knows better than to jump right in but it kills her to have to wait for him to come out with it, she says: so. The son sits, and it makes him smile to look up and he sees her and he sees how anxious his mother is to hear it and to offer something. I don't know, ma, he says. It's not enough of course, but gives her permission to prompt him and asks a simple question about trouble at home, meaning his wife. He says, nothing about her, and he knows she wouldn't understand about the pledge of allegiance. He tells the simple facts of the bus, but finds it harder to explain why he can't tell someone like the old bag to learn some manners and does what he's told. You've just got to tell her to learn some manners, says his mother, and now he feels it with his mother: later he'll have the perfect words to reply but now he's at a loss. I know, ma, he says, but it's his mother and doesn't feel the usual frustration, because of concern. He says I'll work on it, says it with sincerity because he didn't expect his mother to have the answer but it makes him feel better to feel the care of a mother. She says you get out among people and see how they are when they're different from you, she says you'll be surprised. He is surprised, because he doesn't expect this type of remark from his mother. She says you're like your father.

The meaning of different generations: another, but to continue, and it's to repeat, to receive. She must be right but can only remember, for that time, or for now, another place.

THE FIRST CAR YOU REMEMBER was a Ford, they all were, a Ford man like your father would trade in for a new Ford every year, at first. 1950, 51, 2, would stick with Fords till he died when you were in high school, and you had one, 1957 from when he taught you to drive a stick on it. You're reaching as far as you can: his first Fords were round, it's the best word for it, later with sharp fins and "lines," "hot" cars he would drive fast, off the line for a short stretch with just you in the car you could see a teenager in him, but they were family cars because you and your sister made a family. Photos showed your father with his arm around your mother before you were born, home from the navy, and a eagerness was in his eye. You can imagine your father "raising heck" with his buddies staying out all night or you can imagine a passionate night with your mother, 18. It's easy to see in the Fords and how it's in these cars, or now you can see it, a new one every year to preserve something of it, maybe in the back seat, before you were born. But it wore off, you're not sure but there stopped being a new car every year and it meant it couldn't preserve it for him, he had a job and every day he went there and every day he came home, it's what he had to expect. He did but he couldn't have known what it meant. He had two weeks every year and would use it going to another state, where your grandma lived, with you and your sister and your mother and it was a time to drive one of these cars. The first summer when you could have possibly been aware of girls, 11, you had a beautiful cousin at the lake there and "fell in love," actually painfully, pitifully since she was already older. Catching sand-bass with her father in a boat he had, brother of your father's, and his second wife made biscuits-and-gravy. Your father taught your mother to put his jeans on metal stretchers, in the legs, after she washed them to dry and he learned it from this sister-in-law. You remember thinking it meant clothes when you saw a sign that said "whites only" in a laundro-mat. When your father looked at the box of photos, you would get them down to look but he liked to look and he liked to see himself in the old pictures from the navy. It's true, there was a time when he was garrulous but as far back as you can remember he kept to himself, or he would stay in the background. It would be you and your sister in the back seat when you went to drive-in movies with your parents in the old Fords, leaving the drive-in in the clouds of dust and headlights would be shining.

A particular choice, but does a choice escape anything, or can it have its own boundaries? He knew it belonged to him, in two ways. First, and again.

FAMILY ACTIVITY NIGHT at the elementary school, his wife told him, from his son preparing for it at school all week. It was "non-competitive" games. At the pledge of allegiance they were all people who must have believed in secret arms deals or military buildups around the world, but he went and it made a change. Not a change, in fact it made him mad to go, the baby asleep and he would go alone with his son, but he wanted to control this in himself and give something a chance, like the advice of his mother. It was kids and adults in the auditorium and they were all standing on the floor. A man had a microphone at first but he put it down because it was silly, everyone could hear. Something said he was a coach. His job seemed to be to give enthusiasm to everyone, it was in the games he was getting them to do, beginning with just walking, milling would be a better way to put it, until he said stop. You chose the first person in front of you, not a relative, and you went through a series of things together, name, age, etc. Stand on two feet, two people on two feet meant you had to hold on (touching). More touching was the point, and how they would have to cooperate: "join up" with another couple, four people on three feet and two hands, and talking with strangers to work out a way you could. It was clever but he was mad because he didn't want to be in a good mood, when he had to sit down on the floor with his "family members" (son) to talk about a series of things he got pissed at him because he was supposed to be forthcoming and he wouldn't. It was disgusting because he knew his son wouldn't because he sensed how peevish he was, how peevish the father was. The last thing was to arrange themselves, adults with adults, kids with kids, according to birthdays—without talking, form a line of people with birthdays. He tried to be enthusiastic and it satisfied him to find his place and the people around him and he discovered his birthday was the same as two other adults', it almost pleased him. His mother was right but he couldn't admit something or give up something.

This much, but it can stop and he can change something about something, what he receives or how to use it: time, again. Not the first way but the second way, later.

HIS FATHER WOULD GO TO "CONVENTIONS," suits and a suitcase, walking out to a plane with stairs down, and Jack Benny at the airport once and Mickey Mantle would be there once, all the stars. Going up to Jack Benny on the "tarmac" and with a pen for an autograph, how tired he looks and needs a shave. Glancing down, taking the pen to sign it and stabs him with his fingernail, Jack Benny's fingernail, and breaks his skin, he writes his name on a scrap of paper, that looks like a scribble not "Jack Benny," and keeps looking all over the airport like a plane is missing. In a different city, the convention is selling things, insurance, and it was to learn a better way to get a better job. Different companies are there, "firms," and you go by and they interview you for a job—you leave off your résumé—they like it and they interview you for a job. He had a good one and looked good in a good suit but he would talk and it would make him feel stupid, a salesman and selling himself meant he had to lie about it. He flew home and put on khakis and got in his recliner to watch a fight on tv, or put on his khakis and got in the car with the whole family for a drive, it's Sunday and a drive "in the mountains" is nice for everyone. You play games in the back seat of the Ford with your sister and billboards. A job as a mechanic worked out better for the whole family, less money but it was something he wanted and it seemed like it, it would be a good way to remember him and to think of your childhood. Your father would come home dirty with black grease and dirt and if he took a shower he could relax "with the family."

But if you could or if you had the time to, or if your father had the time, something else could be added. A question remains, not a choice.

a
living

▼

IT'S ABOUT THAT he can't get
through, now that he's in there, standing at some kind of attention
you can't talk, or you have to say it all again usually you have to
repeat what you said and how he's going back over things, but
some people don't want to hear it. He has some patience for it
because of his home life, some things about the people there. See
I like to get 2 sanders set up with different grits, use one with 80,
until you're ready for 120, use the other one, you don't spend your
time changing paper, is what makes sense to him. Perfect sense, or
he has an intuition about it that he can't express, and there's no
reason his boss can't see it, it's that it's too simple for words,
natural like when to come out and fire at the clusters of invaders
that appear on the screen. He runs up a high score, his initials are
programed into the video tape for a week at a time. Look he says,
I've been sanding in this shop, I'm the fastest guy you've got. This
means he knows what he is doing.

"You can if you want to look at it that way, Neal. But the reason you're in here is a matter of efficiency. I mentioned the cost of a sheet of sandpaper."

Neal doesn't know whether to give it another try or forget it. If the grit gets dull, he says (loses its sharpness), like anything else when it loses its sharpness, the jointer or a saw blade, if you mention efficiency, thinking of this as a new way to put it. You stand there for fifteen minutes, what do you think's worth more. Or you could think of it as the grit gets clogged, is how you get the swirls.

"The issue is getting as much out of a sheet of sandpaper as you can. Sometimes I pick it up off the floor in there. You could start working with Tom, if you think you'd like to put together drawer-boxes for him, Neal. Or gluing on edges. But we want to see you get your efficiency up first, not just that you know what to do, but that you care about it. I'd rather pay the money out in wages, money in your pocket, too." This about Tom is the thing to say to end the struggle the boss knows, and Neal knows this about what he said, but he goes back out in the shop. Fuck it, he'll use the same piece of fucking sandpaper all day. Maybe the boss was sincere about Tom but what the fuck, he puts foam plugs in his ears, from the deafening machinery and turns on his sander, doesn't have to think about any of this while he's sanding. Down to 120. He can notice the difference in something like tone made by different grits, after all this time: 120 the highest pitch, vibrating the board and his arm and into his head, fine little grits of sand cutting away the roughness left by 80, him humming the same note fills his earplugged head up with vibration.

And it's natural: the more he thinks about this talk with the boss the more it burns him, this statement about working with Tom. They've mentioned it so many times it's their way of getting him back out in the shop or keeping him there that he doesn't even want to work with Tom or anyone anymore. Fuck these people and their cabinets he'll just sand the fucking things and make his paycheck. He wouldn't mind taking a job pumping gas but what's the point, you might as well just take your paycheck, if you don't have to think about anything then what's the problem. This thought makes him feel happy and what he does after work. By the time the 4:00 whistle blows he feels fortunate to have a job that suits him so well, pretty pleased with himself, even to get to give a little grief to his employers from time to time, they all know he would be extremely hard to replace, anyone who could put up with it.

He drives to the arcade carefree and he runs up some high scores but when he goes home one of the girls he lives with is up and he can't get past her but she notices. It's the one who teaches a number of languages, makes a little money here and there from it. Polyglot. It's just that she expects him to sit with her and talk, tell her about his day or some damn thing. So goddamn ugly. It's about that she wants to be a mother or somebody's mother so bad that she cares about him, and he appreciates this of course, but he doesn't enjoy the sex they have. He's careful to not get her pregnant and she hates this, but it's something she says she understands or expects but she wants the sex anyway. Neal doesn't know who else she has sex with but it doesn't make any difference, he feels compassion and they go up to her room and the candle burning. Her body is actually very good, soft and he knows he's not great-looking himself, they do some things that feel incredible on the bed. Always amazed by her slippery wetness inside when he feels it each time it seems like his heart jumps and he hears her moaning her heart beating. He can't get over that she has this hole here that gets wet to make her feel like this, and touching it makes him feel this, his fingers, moving in there. He has to hurry pulling on a rubber sliding in and both arching in, and arching into the thing, arching, so he goes in deeper. In a minute they collapse and Neal collapses on her and his face in her hair on the side. He promised not to leave for his own room until she goes to sleep after it and he never does. He doesn't mind, he likes her enough. The other roommate knows they do it, but they've agreed not to say anything verbally but in the morning he knows he'll have to resist some pressure or a look.

Or he goes straight to his own room where he prefers it where he keeps a photograph, that his mother picked out with him of a store on the corner in her hometown. They had it made into a poster on the wall. She's asleep already on her cot along the wall of the room and she's breathing almost a snore, in and out through her nose and her old slack mouth. Neal knows she'll wake up and she won't remember waking up in the morning because when he comes in she does this. She must be sixty or seventy, never says anything at these times except that they'll have a store like this one on the wall when he, Neal, makes money for it. This is when she wakes up when he comes in but she never remembers. Neal understands that this is her really wanting it even if she never mentions it besides these times she doesn't remember. She'll never have it but he doesn't want to hurt her feelings, he gets under the covers in his bed and turns his back to her to go to sleep instead of saying forget it mother or telling her to shut up. Some people he knows would but he never would say something like that to his mother, who he respects.

His mother doesn't go back to sleep this particular night for some reason keeps talking to him and he understands that she is actually awake this time, something is changed, maybe it makes her think of something but she keeps talking about the store like it was something they always talked about. Until Neal has to turn over to her and he says mother, what is it, he's worried about her, this about how they'll stock the shelves from where they keep the stock in the back in its cardboard boxes, about stamping prices on the cans with purple ink. They must be dusty. What he said makes his mother get a strange look on her face, or the sound of it, like she recognizes something and she stops the thing and lays back down to go to sleep, like she won't remember this in the morning either. She'll be dead by the time they get a store in her hometown, is what she probably realized, 5 bucks an hour. This time Neal gets out of bed though and goes over and tucks the covers around her and kisses her on her wrinkled forehead. Listen mother, he says to his mother asleep on her cot, I had a run-in with my boss today, if you know anything about sandpaper.

She used to get up and make lunch for Neal going to work and the girls that live there but she wasn't so old, to stay on the cot in his room until they've all left now. She doesn't know why, she's tired for all she knows and she won't have to run into them and think of something, might as well spend her time laying there instead, and praying, to god or she likes to pass the time by trying to remember what day it is and what's on tv. She's guilty that she does this and that she can't make their lunch and make a contri-bution. It doesn't matter because of all she's done and she's raised her children by now but her son can at least let her sleep late. She wouldn't mind except for these girls, who she just doesn't know or she tried to get a feel for something about them but they could only talk, she didn't know about what. They move through the house and in the bathroom. But her son seems to like them, because they live together. She couldn't say, one way or the other, decides to sit on the top step of the stairs on the rug and looks down there. They're all gone and she imagines she feels lonesome, how she prefers it because she can rest at least. When she was a young woman she sat alone and felt like this and it fills her with pity or something like disgust to think about it, the young woman who didn't prefer it, needed them all around all the time, her men or some others, to talk to. When she got old there were more people and it got precious to feel this because she learned to get away from them by going in a room, where she would sleep at night where she could get this feeling of being alone. Sometimes she talked to them or sat with them somewhere but she always got up. Later, the girls in this house were always listening to something and she went to her son's room. It was her room, because they shared it, or else she would have gone with her sister. She knows these girls will get home soon because of the shadows because it's time to go lay on her cot while they go in and out of the bathroom taking showers they see each other without their clothes on. She has an urge to see a naked girl sometimes for some reason but it would mean going into something with her and hearing about something.

Instead she goes into her son's room to sit down and to pick up his newspapers to read, that he piles to the ceiling that tell about the world, crime and about the headlines about murders and abuse. She likes to do this on her cot when these girls come home, what they must think about what she's doing in here and she does like to read about it like Neal does, when he buys them about the crime in the city and she's reading about a little girl when Neal walks in. Neal looks embarrassed when he sees his mother, from the sex, or guilty, but she notices and wants to put it behind them, by making him feel better. The only thing she can think of is to challenge him to some cards. It works and Neal feels immediately better from this gesture so they play cards together in the room, deal them out on the cot and they bid against each other. His mother's a pretty good card player, all her marbles and she keeps a count of the cards that have been played, in her head. She's not like some of these other old women with their thin hair. Sometimes she turns her head and makes a mark with a pencil though because she loses track, due to her old age.

But she admits this freely, but you can tell how much she regrets it when it gets late and she has to do this but she doesn't try to hide it. But she knows exactly what she's doing when he plays a card she trumps it but it's so late they don't finish the game before bed. It makes him wish he'd stayed at the arcade longer, to see her struggling like that.

Gun Control

▼

once: desire

SOME BENT BIRDS seem like survivors and below them nothing is moving, the only sound is a cicada, on a hot day and the humidity, and a man can hear his own footsteps on a road. Crops destroyed by a flood from a river and crooked brown stalks sticking up from the mud and the muddy fields, he tosses a rock out into it, it makes a sound like a sodden sound when it hits. A building looks like a ruined farm-house from the filthy flood and an Army helicopter flies up from behind it, all of a sudden, he watches from where he's standing on the road and it looks like a woman's underclothes like a white slip accidentally dangling from underneath. But it flies off away from him in the other direction and he can't get a better look, but he wanted to: he can't get over it, what he can see from the flood of a powerful river, and walking along for two days and the old canvas bag with his stuff along the edges of a major flood, notices the details of ruined things, and sleeps on sandbags and he can beat them into a comfortable shape for his body at night. He's been trying to imagine the violence, raging mud of the water and the action of it, but it's over and it's all silence and makes him feel cheated, studies the shape of outbuildings on a farm and the current twisted or pushed them into another shape, in the middle of acres of wasted mud.

At first, he saw what the flood left when he came up on it, and he had a desire to and two times he went off the road into it to cross the battered fields. But the smooth silt of mud on top sucked his boots down and forced him back to the road, and he'd look out into it staring out, and had to start trying to imagine something about it. Now he wants to get out to the house and see what the helicopter left, white rectangle of floor-boards, surrounded by mud, where the dresser was in the bedroom, but knowing the impossibility of it would make him go back to the road. He's thinking and he thinks he might find a dead telephone, pick up the receiver or wipe dried mud off the controls of a tractor. He wonders what it would be like to be dragged under water. The next day he counts fifteen mud-covered mounds and they're drowned cows.

his authority, his project

A MAN BUILT A CORRUGATED COVER from rain between the screen door of his kitchen and the uninsulated shed for a workshop, where he stood and he looked out into the dark rain at night in the direction of the confluence of two big rivers, and drinking coffee he made, big cup sweet with sugar. The man was no fool, he made sure to build his place high enough up on the bluff that the rivers wouldn't ever get up to it if and when they flooded, he had enough land to and he knew better, standing by and drumming a rhythm on a four-by-four upright and he was thinking, or remembering: piling sandbags into the mud of the bank of the road, that he took from somebody who fed them down to him, a tall kid that got them out of a pickup, and some-one asked about livestock and his corral. He didn't break his stride or look up, but told them no, not his corral, he said build your own, he said there's plenty of high ground. He was happy to do his share with the sandbags. But he stopped, he stood up and he looked them in the face and stood there looking and that was all, he took the next sandbag, it gave him the feeling of a machine, grabbing the bag by two burlap corners, swinging them with his body into the mud bank and moving down the line.

He went in the workshop standing on the hard-packed floor, dirt and he put his coffee down on a workbench. Two loading-presses were bolted to the front of the bench and a vice on the end, wooden jaws that held the roughed-out stock of a rifle. Chisels on the bench next to the stock, different sizes and a mallet and a wood-rasp, he put them in a drawer under the wooden top of the workbench and drank some coffee, reaching up and he turned on a tv above the bench. His place gets the only clear picture in the township and while it warmed up he lit a gas flame under a pot of cold lead and changing the dies in a loading press, for lead bullets and the heat started turning the metal to liquid. On tv a Western came on and he turned it up and measuring black gunpowder into .44mm brass cases out of a cigar box, a precise amount from a triple-beam balance and lined them up on the bench. The lead in the pot then melted and he lifted the scum off the top of the molten metal with a piece of paraffin and he began to dip it out with a wooden-handled ladle and fill bullet molds.

pain, tolerance

TWENTY MILES UP RIVER in Pacific City, Claire raises her fingertips to her bruised cheek, thinking about what Dale told her before some unknown thing set him off. She reaches for the glass of brown whiskey next to the bed and rests back on a feather pillow. Music is on, on a radio on a table against the wall.

He was chewing food, talking about it, talking about a kid. Claire watched the muscles in his temples when he chewed but she didn't know why he was talking about it or what it meant, or should she ask about it. What do you mean?

Dale said I don't mean anything, there was a damn kid, looked like some college type kid.

On the Fork road?

He looked at her face, took another drink, eating, watching Claire he said yeah, Claire. She didn't look at his eyes fixed on her but watched his jaw and it's muscles and his flat cheeks. What'd I say, Claire, walking out on the Fork road, carrying one of these duffel bags, with a strap on it. He washed down a mouthful of food with whiskey, and on the counter an open cardboard case of bottles of whiskey.

What was a kid doing there? She said it but then she knew it was a bad thing to say. Dale stopped chewing, and called her something vulgar. How the fuck am I supposed to know that, Claire?

twice: to penetrate

HE HEARS A MOTORCYCLE'S ENGINE before he sees it, and the white smoke of a motorcycle behind him and first thinks to duck behind sandbags, because by now it's important, to be alone, keep going into the disaster of a flood. But he decides not to and he wants to see who it is and thinks he wants to find out, or to find something. He hasn't talked to anyone since he came down off the hill, so he stands, and facing the motorcycle coming. But a black motorcycle, no muffler, gets closer, and he decides to be visible might be a mistake but it's too late.

Dale lets off the throttle when he sees a man on the road up ahead, he's thinking and he figures it must be somebody the Corps of Engineers left behind, slows up and he stops across the road from the kid, he has a glove on and he's squeezing the brake with his hand, looks into his blue eyes across the road. Neither one says anything but they stare at each other, for a long time, it seems like a long time and the motorcycle engine is revving. Dale sees the kid's foot move on the road, finally, with his eyes and pops the Indian's clutch, throwing dirt and rocks back behind him and off down the road, heads to the place up the bluff, where he goes.

Watching the motorcycle go off down the road and he runs his fingers through his hair and picks up the canvas bag, starts after it. Later the black machine passes him going back and without slowing down.

domestic violence

GREG WAS STANDING in the red glow behind the idling van taking a leak. He noticed that the bulb above the license plate had burned out, made a note to replace it. In the front seat, his wife was saying something he couldn't hear. He returned to the driver's side, pulling on his fly. The door was open.

"Did you say something?"

"I said I don't think you know what you're talking about, Greg. According to this we should have seen some kind of town by now. I really think we ought to just turn around and plan on spending the night at that little turn-off." Greg had stopped the van so his wife could read the map again. He personally saw no need to.

"I'm not sure I could find it again."

"Well, how do you know the road's not completely washed out up ahead? We should have paid attention to those signs, Greg, damnit. I don't want to spend another night parked on the road."

"Lucy, I know what I'm doing, okay? The first thing these people do when it floods is sandbag this road so the wheat won't get flooded. Will you please just trust me? Martin used to live here." He took the tire gauge to the back of the van, found that one tire was four pounds low. As he stood up, pushing the calibrated bar back into its housing, he thought he heard a motorcycle. He listened but he couldn't figure it out: the sound seemed to be coming to him from the direction of the river.

"That's funny," he said to his wife, handing her the tire gauge. "I could have sworn I heard a motorcycle or something off in the direction of the river."

"Let's get out of here, Greg. This place gives me the creeps."

"Aw, Luce, it was just a trick my ears were playing on me. This place does that. It plays with you. That's what I used to love about it."

"Goddamnit, Greg."

again: to touch

A DESERTED TOWN at the confluence of two rivers, he came into it when it got dark and sat down on planks on a mud-covered porch, from a clean-up crew and sat watching light flicker in a window up the bluff, decided to stay there, where he was, spend the night in this building because it was a building muddy water tore through, he could use his imagination. He had a flashlight, and standing up shined a beam of light onto a plywood path of boards that led through the door off its hinges, like the mouth of a cave and the sound of watery mud under the plywood when he stepped on it. At the edge of a sheet of plywood he kneeled and pushing his open hand into mud and it covered his knuckles, bent his fingers and scraped the floor and this would force fine sand under his nails. Laying down on his back and he let the mud dry on his hand, he couldn't figure something out, the motorcycle, the man on it, on his way to this deserted town on the road but he couldn't guess why or what for, to do something. They looked at each other for a long time on the road, motorcycle revving, and then shot off and like he dismissed him, he spent an hour then figuring to come up on him stopped on the road and examining what was left of a flood-damaged Corvair or measuring a water-mark, a building, and the idea of salvaging a building. Finally realizing the man took another road, going into the hills on his way to some secret place, but the machine appeared then suddenly over a rise in the road, speeding past, why? He left his duffel bag on the plywood to go back out to the porch with his hands in his jean pockets and looking up the hill. A long time later he went back into the building and came back out with the flashlight, found a plywood path across the main street and began the climb up.

toward self-worth

CLAIRE STANDS BEHIND THE SCREEN watching the big shape of her husband kick his motorcycle started. His broken leather boot coming down with force onto the metal starter excites her. Briefly, she touches herself. She watches him drive away from her on the machine and she blows cigarette smoke through the screen, she says the son-of-a-bitch and she thinks it's something like rage. Claire has given up trying to convince Dale to stop spending time at the place on the bluff. She doesn't know but she understands his need, from his clenched jaw when he turns the throttle with his hand. She knows about the long knife blade at the foot of the bed under the box springs and she sees his face when he comes home, the satisfaction, silent and drunk, at night.

Claire pours sour mash into a jelly glass and right away drinks off half, she likes the way it burns on the way down her throat. It's been two days and she's been alone. She decides to walk out onto the ridge when she finishes the whiskey, sit with her arms hugging her knees and watch the tractors. They'll be gone by the end of the week, when they finish pushing the flood back into the river. She lets her legs spread beneath the table and puts two fingers into the amber liquid then into her mouth, sucking the sweet taste.

then: to receive

HE ISN'T SURPRISED, finding a motorcycle like the other one and it's leaning against the side of the barn, stands by it and he touches the dirty fender with his hand, grabs the throttle and he waits and he turns it a little, smell of unburned gasoline in his nostrils, and he closes the throttle. He puts his hand on the seat and it's cracked vinyl, and picks dried mud off the tank with his fingernails. When he began earlier climbing the dark climb up the bluff, and pointing his flashlight at bushes and plants and round stones and he came out on a road, worn tire tracks separated by a mound of growth, angling up the bluff and heard the first gunshot of the night. It made him jump back into the brush, and sitting for half an hour and picking off leaves off bushes, with his fingers, he heard a pattern of a gun firing and for a long time it didn't stop, shots, finally he went back out on the road and decided to follow it. Standing now with his back to the motorcycle and looking out at the overgrown weeds in a barnyard, and another gunshot. He gets down and holding the luggage rack above the back tire, he's listening to the regular pattern of gunshots, it starts up again, goes around the barn and back in the woods and comes up on the house from the other side and hugging up against clapboard, edges around. He sees the back of a man, black clothes and a hat and he looks around the last drainpipe into the shed, crawling along the edge of a wooden porch and gets a good view. He watches and a man with a wide-brimmed black hat, crouches and behind him a color television blinking and holds his hand open at his side, face pushed out forward, rigid body turned back at an angle, like running but with his left hand he reaches up to touch his hat-brim, takes it and pulls it down to an angle. His right hand, he releases it, thumb moving on the hammer as soon as his palm touches the rough grip and his back muscles tense and his right shoulder coming up, elbow bends, and the barrel clears his leather holster, body dips, follows the forward thrust of the .44 and as soon as the black barrel levels he fires into a pile of sandbags across the room.

you take what you can

GREG WAS PISSED when he finally had to admit they couldn't go any further than the edge of the town of Defiance. He left his wife in the parked van and walked into the dark town on the paths of dirty two-by-tens and sheets of half-inch plywood that covered the silt. He briefly considered trying to drive the van on these wooden paths—Greg hates to have to retrace his steps and choose another route. It seems like such a waste; it makes him feel foolish. When he returned to the van, he was prepared to direct his anger at his wife. He climbed into the driver's seat without speaking, started the engine.

"Well?"

Greg stuck his head out the window in order to back the van. "Take the flashlight and get out behind me. I can't tell how close I am to that damn ditch."

Lucy stood at the edge of a small ditch holding a flashlight. She gestured when the van was close, climbed back in. "Do you think you can find that turn-off?"

Greg hadn't succeeded in turning the van around yet, was backing again. When he had backed as far as he dared, he shifted into first, kept the clutch depressed, looked at his wife's face lit up by the green lights under the dash. "We'll figure something out, Lucy. Okay?"

"I just don't like the idea of spending the night parked on the road, Greg."

He wished he could have thought of a way to reply to a remark like that—its tone made him want to punch her. That would be the thing—just haul off and smack her one, without saying a word. Instead he lit a thin cigar, threw the match out the window, avoided looking at her. He let off the clutch, moved slowly along the damaged road.

Ed

▼

SOME PEOPLE DROVE UP and
he got in, thinking he could phone later and say where he'd gone,
where he remembered a payphone, and say that he had agreed to
go with them, after all. It seemed natural that he could call when
they got where they were going. It's important to think of these
things, but he couldn't keep his mind on it and he climbed in, old
truck, their old van rather, and with windows and it had out-of-
state plates, still, and a bumper sticker, and he noticed climbing
in that someone had thought to put a piece of old carpet in the
back. Something like that can make all the difference.

He was glad to be in there, as always, it was pleasant and they
all said hello to each other, and they drove away as soon as he was
inside, to stop somewhere else first: the reason everyone was in
such exceptionally good spirits, he was figuring it out, simply
asking, and it didn't bother him to ask and he would find out
where they were going first, or there wasn't any of the usual
smoking to get high, but everyone was in a good mood because

they were on their way to pick some up. It was a good errand, but it took some time.

Driving, and by now he was riding up front, it was pretty far out of the way so he reached over and switched on the tape player, jazz on a tape, or rock-and-roll, something, but something they'd like. He didn't know how long it would take, and just wanted to make it comfortable in the van (thinking he'd wait in the van when they got there). It turned out to be alright, everyone appreciated the music and listening made them anticipate getting high, afterwards, on the way through town. Think of listening to this stoned, they said. It was a great relief to him that this gesture of his was appreciated, from feeling like a part of the group, and the reason it felt immediately pleasant in the van earlier, the hello's and so on. This is not what he had in mind when he turned the tape on, he hoped this was clear, but he felt encouraged to include himself when they pulled into the suburban driveway.

He'd never been in a house like this one before, and feeling like part of the group today, of course, in the first place, and being able to assert himself, to see it. Because he just said he'd rather come in with them, and of course it didn't matter, and they didn't care—it was just him and his nervousness.

It was one of these ranch houses in the suburbs, with a lawn, and polished wood furniture. The houses sprawl out there, it's a good word to describe how it looks, the houses are so low and this one had a roof that sloped ever-so-gently, with lawn mowers next to the parked car through the open door of the garage, for two cars, and he could imagine a chemistry set in there. In fact, it was a young woman in her late twenties that opened the door and he could imagine that she had a son the right age, and selling ounces, this is what they wanted to buy, from her. That is, they knew this—she was somebody's friend.

It was all very casual, out there in the suburbs. They had some

tea with her in the large kitchen, nobody acted like they were
buying dope. He gathered her husband bought a half-pound from
someone where he worked, in construction: a contractor, who
made a lot of money apparently, because of the fine furniture in
the living room—anyone can buy a half-pound occasionally. And
some other things.

This is something he had misunderstood, that is, she had
mentioned a contractor but he seemed to be someone else's
husband, or at least not hers, but he didn't find out until later,
and he was considering not to leave with them, in their van.
Because he got the idea she was attracted to him—this is something he was interpreting. But she didn't mean anything like that
either, it was a disappointment but she was being battered by her
husband and she was simply trying to think of a way to prevent
him from doing this to her, when he got home, figuring, if
someone else was there. It became quite a problem for them. He
didn't know what to do, but he had misunderstood about this
husband, and hoping she would just accept it that he couldn't
very well stay with her under these circumstances, they all did,
but they wanted her to tell them the story, at least, and they'd
stick around and help her out as much as they could (if she would
tell it it helps). No one wanted to suggest she call the police—you
never know, in these situations.

Then she told them this story, and it was true. The husband
wasn't supposed to drink, and she said she had a court order,
which she wanted to show them but didn't, for some reason, so
they didn't know what it said. The kids she said were her kids
from a previous marriage, it happened that this was their time to
get home from school, or the babysitter (a look in their eyes and
their eyes darted and they didn't say anything to them and they
walked through). The new husband had hit the little girl when he
was drunk recently and this was when the woman got a court

order, but now it was Friday afternoon and she knew he'd been drinking beer after work with his buddies as she called them, although they were actually only his co-workers, drinking six-packs after the job. She said she was afraid to be home alone if he came home drunk—he'd slapped her around, too, it was a very ugly situation, and she didn't stop smoking cigarettes the whole time. She referred to herself as battered.

Needless to say, everyone felt terrible after seeing those two kids. But it was an awful dilemma. You don't want to involve yourself, as much as you'd like to do something, but there are shelters and things of that nature that are much better equipped, and they all started worrying about what kind of a scene it would cause, with them there, if he came home now, and what could they possibly say, an explanation seemed out of the question. Of course, they knew this wasn't the point and it made him, for one, feel extremely guilty, but she began insisting they leave and she was putting a good face on it. It was clear to her what a bad scene it would be, because she had only been entertaining a wild hope, she said, or something, and said last time she'd taken the smallest child with her to a neighbor. It had been pretty embarrassing, she said, though, because the neighbor had company over—a couple with an infant and you could tell how anxious they were for the police to arrive. She walked them to the door, huge glass sliding doors onto the side patio. And they shuffled nodding to the van and stood wishing her luck and goodbye for a minute, before they started it up.

They were on their way now, again, and she was standing in the two-car driveway watching. It was a shame, but he supposed she went to the neighbor's.

Nobody could bring himself to talk about fishing, or on the drive out there for a long time. Because they were smoking now, holding their breath, and getting high and thinking about what had just happened, or what they could do but it made them feel helpless. And he couldn't stop thinking about the idea that he could just as well have waited in the van, or what if he had decided not to come along today at all? He couldn't help thinking about this, once he got started, because it actually had crossed his mind not to come today. But he always enjoyed standing around the fishing pond with them, their lines angle down from the tips of their poles into the water.

It was a windy day and some new people were at the fishing pond, some others from the city. There was a young couple in their teens, who had their stuff on a picnic table behind them, their portable radio and it was playing AM music, top 40, made it a tender scene, the way he would show her how to hold her pole out so the bait could get into the current, what little there was. Finally he realized that one of them had a little brother and sister and that these were the kids that kept running over the small rise into the parking lot of the swimming pool. It was fairly simple to figure out—the two kids kept running up to the teenage couple. And two men wearing Levis who started off next to each other, fishing in the same spot, but they both moved away from that spot in a little while, to two different spots, keeping this up, moving to new spots all around the fishing hole and almost all the way out to where the strong current was flowing. These events made him happy they'd claimed their own spot, so to speak, next to the footbridge because they just wanted to stand around with their lines in the water, probably until one of them caught some-thing worth keeping.

People kept looking at them from the footbridge, on their way to the swimming pool, and it was surprising, this late in the season, and he was surprised it was still open, and murmuring something about being surprised, it was a strange thing. He was watching a man, and he had a small baby attached to his chest, an infant hanging in one of those carriers that have become so popular with young parents, and the man was watching the fishermen.

He caught a fish then, all of a sudden, first the feeling of a nibble, of the fish nibbling at his bait, but giving the fish an instant, to take the bait into his mouth and he gave his line a jerk, jerking with a firmness to set the fishhook, in the fish's mouth, and it did, because he felt the line tense immediately, and the fish took off. It wasn't a big one, though, because all he did was reel it in, very easily. Of course, the people he was with were cheering him on, and he was feeling the usual excitement. This was the case whenever one of them got a fish on his line—it wasn't a situation for catching what would be called a big fish, although occasionally they'd catch one big enough to keep, and eat. But there was an excitement from just getting one on your line, and everyone felt it, the anticipation was would it be big enough to keep, and this fish was, and eat, or would it get away.

The fish was flapping the air, hanging on the end of his line, when he lifted it up out of the water, into the air. He flipped it up onto the bank, in the dirt, and it flopped around there and dirt got all over the fish, where it was wet, and little rocks. This made it very unpleasant to touch the fish, when he picked it up, and it still kept struggling back and forth in his hand. He got a rock in his other hand, and decided to kill the fish and not let it drown in the air, struggling like it was, so he hit it on the head with his rock. But this didn't kill the fish, he didn't know how hard to hit it, it kept flopping in his hand and its sharp fins so he hit it on the head again, harder, and one more time, even, harder than that. And of course it finally stopped struggling, and flopping, and he was free to let go of it so it hung twisting around, on his line. He wiped his hand off on his pants, the dirt from the ground when the fish had been flopping down there.

He had to free his hook by cutting the line, inside the fish's mouth, and did this with his nail clippers, and pushing the hook all the way through, in the same direction as it had gone into the flesh. If you do this, it eventually comes back around, and out a new spot instead of pulling out a lot of flesh with the hook if you pull back, against the barb.

Finally he took the fish into the brush down where the river was flowing, to clean it. You feel as if you're going to the bathroom, going down there, with a fish in your hand. Someone had loaned him a very sharp hunting knife and it was so sharp that he just opened the belly of the fish from its neck to its tail very easily, with a stroke. And exposed his organs and what's inside, the stomach and you can recognize the little yellow kidneys. But most of it looks like liver and there's some blood involved. If you reach up into the cavity, towards the fish's head, and find what is either an air pipe or the esophagus or some little tube, most of the insides of the fish will usually come out fairly easily, if you pull this down and where everything is attached to the inside of the back, work it out with your thumbnail on the way down. He left the fish's insides for some animal, in the brush next to the river.

Parental Authority

▼

1. Despite your best intentions.

IT'S NOT WHAT MY MOTHER calls it because I still care about my kids, that's the reason and it's just that she can't understand. I care about my kids, but some things about my life make it impossible, and like it is for now, what it means to be a parent. She can't understand something though, about it, but I told her the story again and I said it wouldn't be forever, it isn't a long time. But it seems like it to her and she thinks of it like that.

I said ma, I'll tell you again. My mother is old, it's hard for her, but I told her I was destroying my kids. I've been alone with two kids: except for a short time after my husband, living with a man for a short time, I've been by myself with them since one boy was less than three, and the other one a baby. This is ten years. I told this story again to my mother: I was driving a panel truck cross country in the winter with my two kids, she remembers this part because I stayed with my sister for half a year in my home town. The truck was old and the heat worked but there were holes in the body and sometimes it wouldn't start. I was nursing the baby and I would stop but I didn't want to turn off the engine. I kept driving because I didn't have enough to stay in motels, in the glove compartment someone let me borrow a gun and I could see it because the glove compartment would pop open if I hit a bump. I said, ma, it's better for them to go away for awhile, I thought it through, I have to get control of my life.

I took some bourbon.

I was living in Oregon with some people, in a small town, my first baby was born and midwives were there, I had him at home. No one I knew went to a hospital. A lot of people were midwives and a lot of women were having babies, the process of birth was important to women. Men were involved and they would be there, men and women would go through it together, pregnancy, but there's something—birth belongs to a woman and other women would help in the birth, a man could hold your hand and his support makes all the difference, but another woman knows where to put her hands and she can open things up like a man can't. And she can check and she knows the feeling of a live baby coming out, and of course a man can't know how this feels either. I don't mean to imply blame, but birth was important to the women I knew in Oregon, and a man should go through it with a woman, it's important.

A man was my husband and when my first boy was born he went through it with me, some exercises and we'd practice during pregnancy, breathing exercises every day, and preparing yourselves for the experience of birth. Sharing these things made us closer, and I believe this is common for couples when they have a baby, the birth process seemed to make our friends closer.

We had a baby, then. And I remember when he was born,

after the hours of pushing and bearing down, a wet baby with some fluids and some blood, but I put him immediately to my breast and my nipple seemed so big for his little mouth. It upset me when he didn't suck right away because I thought it would be the first thing he'd want, you just figure the whole thing must have made him pretty hungry, or they say they're traumatized. Or it's not that but I wanted him to rejoin me physically, with my nipple in his mouth like a desire. But other women reassured me and told me it took some time for a baby to figure it out, what to do. Of course I knew this from talking to others and I had been at several births and the baby never just latches right on, but I guess I wanted something ideal.

In two years when I got pregnant again, my husband didn't go through it with me, he changed. Things got worse, I was sick a lot during my second pregnancy and my husband would get pissed if I couldn't make my son be quiet, he was two, if he cried. There was outrage during those months, my boy would cry when my husband yelled, and slamming out of the house yelling. He wasn't there even, for the birth, it was because I told him not to be, it was over. He muttered something. Some friends helped as much as they could, and I left Oregon soon after the baby was born.

2. Despite your best intentions.

ELEVEN YEARS OLD meant it was time for it, and a man knew it was time for naked pictures of women but he came home unexpectedly and the boy had his friend over and in the bathroom of the small apartment, the pictures were cut out of magazines and on the floor. He wanted to say something to make him feel better but he was a bad parent, smiling and the friend ran home, the boy picked them up and hurried to his room, you couldn't ignore it, it meant a talk in the boy's room. He said some things, he didn't know what to say he said it's okay he said look, I understand this because all boys do something like this, and so did I. He wanted to tell the boy about when he was a kid and his friend was next door, his house and the friend's house, some dirt in between. Two-bedroom houses and sharing bedrooms with sisters, he can remember the water running in the gutter of the street, overflow from sprinkler systems and kitchen sinks, kids would dam it up, dirt and some rocks and they would build it higher out into the street but the dam always gave in to the water, washed down the street with the water.

Together with his friend going to the empty field at dusk, weeds and lizards live there it's where he and the others could have rock fights, throwing rocks of different sizes as big as a golf ball, not quite, and you'd get hit with a rock. It hurt but different friends are on different sides and you want it to hurt but nobody wants to get hurt bad. Blood was good but a rock might cause too much blood, in the field and throwing it too hard made them mad. But it was scary and it was exciting to hear a rock hit the dirt nearby and it could've hit you like a bullet. Friends were on the same side but it would start getting dark, it was over, throwing one last rock in the dusty darkness.

With his friend he would move aside certain trash or litter and a big rock, a magazine stolen from a drugstore was damp by now with dirty pages, but the pictures. And stealing it made it theirs in a special way. He wanted to tell the boy about the pictures but not the stealing. The boy's face was hard with mistrust though and the man couldn't say anything: it's alright. It's alright, okay? And he left the room without an answer, in a minute. But he wasn't a good parent because he didn't know how to make this go away and make something better, he was afraid because he wasn't doing it right and it wasn't his son. The man

didn't have a wife and he didn't have a son, but he used to live
with him and he had affection for him, he should live with him.
He wanted to and he did, but he didn't know the consequences
of a single parent.

3. Despite your best intentions.

AND I WOULD TAKE MY BOYS to visit my sister after that, my
older sister, and her husband, and it seemed like a mistake but
I didn't know if it was a mistake in a big house in the suburbs
because her husband was a lawyer, and with a big family with
three kids, counting a new baby, four. My boys would be shy
though, their life and what I had to do with it, as a single parent,
and my sister's house and her oldest boy, the same age as my son
and my other son was still young. But it took a long time to talk,
the best thing was to wait for lunch and my sister's kids wanted
to swim in the pool but my son didn't have a suit, the cousin had
one but I could understand, he didn't want to borrow someone
else's swimming suit, like their underwear. His brother didn't
mind then, younger, but my older boy stuck to me and my
mother was to watch the kids outside like Oregon, after Oregon
but looking for a job, it meant I had to support my own kids,
and someone to watch the kids, I had to work, pulling up in the
truck and it was a long drive with two little kids and leaving my
husband behind me, nursing the baby and I couldn't turn off
the engine. My mother said that's fine, but made sure I knew I
couldn't stay there, two kids, she told me in a letter and she knew
I would stay with my sister, my sister's husband didn't mind, at
first, and my mother didn't mind watching my kids, I went to
work. Until I could get on my feet, a babysitter for my kids but
my mother watches my sister's kids by the swimming pool.

Lunch was soon, or not a long time to wait and my sister wanted
to tell me about a new position or an opportunity for her husband, but I could never remember what position the husband
had or wanted, and it seemed like I was supposed to, or what it
meant, except an amount of money and it didn't make sense that
more would make a difference, like rich people.

My sister thought it would, though, and her husband thought
so, with something to show like an addition or a new swimming
pool and we had to pay attention like my father standing over us,
when I was a girl and with my sisters, it was someone's turn for a
shower and his disgusting body against you, or another time
someone forgot to flush, he pointed and we had to look, we knew
it was him but he was our father and it meant it would be one of
us. I wasn't going to admit something though, this time, to end it
again or to take off my clothes and we were standing there a long
time, my father would rant about something and he might hit us
with his hand, ranting because nobody said anything, a long time
until my sister finally says it's her and it's over, for me and for my
other sister, who must be too young, still. Later, we were in our
room and she came in and sobbing with her swollen eyes and said
why didn't you admit it. She said she did, but she did it because
she was just trying to end it, when we were standing there. I said
it wasn't me. Now my sister's husband is a lawyer.

He took us into the new addition and an automatic sliding
glass door behind us like a shopping mall, a room and it was
empty but it was filled with toys for the young kids, everything,
and toys like a computer and video games for the nephew in a
"loft," stairs and following him up the stairs, my sister's husband,
he told us to sit on a soft rug and urged us to sit down and my
son could play a game, but he didn't want to, he said that's okay,
and I saw him look at the husband, his eyes a second, the things
on the floor and his hands in his pockets, a jean jacket I bought

him, and I saw him pull his hand out and rubbing the side of his nose and to look at his finger and put it back in his pocket. I didn't know what to say but I saw my son, he put his hand back in his pocket, or why I was pissed but I always felt something like that at my sister's house, I couldn't help it though, and I knew it was the computers and games, I was mad and it seemed like it was my sister, but it didn't make sense and I had to keep it inside, my son let me take his hand.

My son's video game broke, he liked to play it at home, sometimes, and with the man I used to live with after work but he wasn't very good and the boy always won. He liked it, though, and the man liked it and it seemed like they had a good time with each other, pushing the buttons and the controls and playing the video game. It broke, the machine for the game broke once, and the man and my boy tried to fix it, a shop said it was too old so they did something to it by themselves with parts all over the apartment and something worked and the game worked if they left the controls plugged in, black electrical tape did this, but they could still play it, black, shiny tape. My sister's kids had every game you could buy or imagine to buy and when a new game came out my sister would buy it or her husband would buy it for their kids, I don't know what they did with all the old games but they separated their trash, they were careful people. They could throw the games away.

At lunch I tried to put it behind me and my sister asked a question about my job, I was glad to have a chance to tell them about a new grant we wrote, for more clients, and more services for people. Her husband would say, does something like that get you a promotion? One of their kids was in the first grade. My sister said they'd have a graduation celebration, but I didn't want to come, fifty people would come. My mother said why don't you come, you should bring the boys.

4. Despite your best intentions.

THE MAN WOULD TAKE THE BOY to visit his mother and a little car could make it across country with him and the boy when they drove through the night, and back, the man couldn't afford a new car but they did it a number of times to visit and his brother was there visiting, the boy's brother would fight with him but they liked to see each other and they liked to play games with each other. Stopping at different truck-stops on the way, night-time and the big trucks parked in lines like a book he used to read to the boy when he was younger, and he was living with his mother. But they were all running, the boy didn't know why somebody didn't steal a big truck and the man didn't know why but he said it's better to leave them running, a diesel. They always filled a thermos with black coffee for the man, and they liked candy, both of them got a candy bar after a hamburger or breakfast, stopping at truck-stops but they were driving straight through, it was the best way to get there in a hurry, he said why draw it out, and the boy was happy to sleep in the car, every once in a while he got tired, but he wanted to, he wanted to see his mother.

They stopped to take a leak, it was before the sun went down but it was dark enough to stand by the side of the road, a stream of pee goes down, in the weeds. A building like a big farmhouse seemed deserted and a pleasant evening, crickets and a cool night, breeze. The man finished and turned around on his way back to the car but the boy said no, wait a minute, he looked back, over his shoulder. He said, what's wrong. Nothing, he said look, pointing in the air, little birds if you could see them, darting around, a field of high weeds and over the field and trees around it but it was strange, a bird, black, darting with fluttering wings, but they were bats, and the boy said they were bats. The man looked and found one, with his eyes, he said you're right! He said what are bats doing out here, and they were amazed, watching the bats for a long time and they were pointing out a bat when it appeared darting up and down and from place to place in the trees and the open field, how many bats at the same time before one's gone, another one appears. The man said I wonder where they came from, and the boy was thinking, he said I bet they live in that farmhouse.

A flashlight from the glove compartment, by now it was dark and it was dark in the deserted house, it must be abandoned, they needed it in there. It gave them the creeps but they were rational about bats, the boy's friend used to have bats for pets and the man worked with bats in college for awhile, in a room. They had to climb the stairs, looking around there were no bats on the first floor but they climbed up and in the bedroom and pointing the flashlight at the ceiling and the bats were hanging on the ceiling, a hundred bats blinded by the light and it seemed like it made them squirm around: bats can't see with their shiny eyes, so it didn't, but they make a high-pitched sound for danger, some flew in the window and some bats flew out but most of the bats were hanging on the ceiling above their heads, 4 or 5 feet, and a lot or most had young bats attached to them, nursing their young. They watched, the bats had thin ears and it seemed like their wings were folded, but they had hands, somehow. The boy was pointing the light at them, he said we should leave them alone. They kept looking but finally walking down the stairs and out and using the flashlight to see the steps and they got back in the car. The man started the car and drove on the highway, but it was a special place, the boy said I can hardly wait to tell Mom.

5. Despite your best intentions.

Her younger sister, she wanted her to stay in their bedroom, the father, and her sister was too young, she didn't think her sister knew everything and she didn't want her to know about the father, ranting at them but a little kid might say something embarrassing, at school or they had friends, sometimes her older sisters take their clothes off. She went to her sister's apartment, living with her boyfriend and to visit, she was leaving in the driveway later and with her sons in the car. The sister said, have you called Dad? She said no. Her sister said you should call him, he'd like to hear from you. She said look, he doesn't want to hear from me, okay.

Blinking Elvis and the Invention of Violence: a True Story

▼

THERE WAS SOMETHING
irrevocable about hitting a child, the two times Blinking Elvis had
slapped a child, something measured but at the last instant it has
to be spontaneous, impulsive—you wouldn't do it. And both
times made it seem like not a bad idea, but Blinking Elvis knew it
was a bad idea. Because things got immediately better when the
kid each time, when both kids responded immediately with a
period of fondness and respect for his authority—or because he
acted, and with the authority of an action, and you respect it
when someone can. But luckily for everyone involved, Blinking
Elvis understood that to simply continue hitting the kids would—
to develop a habit of hitting them—would be to act without
authority, a thing you do and you do it because nothing else
comes to mind. He thought about hitting his wife, but so does
everyone, even if they don't hit children and some do, some

people hit their wives, some for good reasons, and for some men this becomes a habit and for others it seems to happen only once in a while. But in either case such domestic violence is nothing more than the manifestation of something, a type of disruptive energy that solves nothing, even if something that abusive could be absorbed into the habitual life of the family, and seems natural, like hitting would. Somehow Blinking Elvis knew all this. But with kids it's obvious an adult, in his capacity as parent (the idea of a parent) and it would give him a certain responsibility to them, and this takes the form of observing their behavior, making judgments about its appropriateness—for example drugs—and he must maintain, somehow, the authority to correct offensive behavior, it implies they respect that authority. Blinking Elvis found that a measured but impulsive slap to the face insured this respect.

Three times. That is, he actually deliberately slapped children a total of three times in his role as parent (I didn't mention a second time for reasons that will become obvious, and the times he kicked the waifs or urchins that threw dirt into his hair and bit him on the leg as he made his way through the park in the evenings, these encounters being beyond the scope of the present narrative). The second time, intoxicated by his unexpected success at winning the respect of the small girl who received the, it would be wrong to say benefit, of the first slap, and it taught him the absolute necessity of an impulsive blow that was at the same time carefully *measured*. On this occasion, unrestrained by mature reflection, Blinking Elvis had simply "let fly" when, the desirable effects of their first violent encounter exhausted (it should be said that this child was not, as the expression is, Blinking Elvis's own—literally, he was not the biological parent—but he married her mother, whose divorce freed her to take up this relationship with Blinking Elvis and it creates the impression he's the other parent. Her name was Agatha (the child, and such a name should say something about the parents), given to fits of temper which sometimes took the form of rejecting the artificial relationship which, from the point of view of Agatha's mother and Blinking Elvis, entitled Blinking Elvis to a share of authority), defiantly challenged Blinking Elvis's dinner-time reprimand, the issue was her peas, and twisting her face into an expression of utter contempt at his authority enraged him, and the thought of his earlier success, his anger made him lean over the dinner table and a slap excessive in its force and snapped her head to the side, the sharp intake of breath and a wail that makes it clear to Blinking Elvis just how inappropriate it had been to hit her, and didn't dare look at the mother but it pissed him off. Why should he have to feel guilty if this method of discipline had been so successful the first time, and approved in subsequent discussions with Agatha's mother. Of course, Blinking Elvis's anger was a defensive gesture, because of his culpability—the abuse of his overwhelming physical advantage—(at six-foot-one, he weighed over two-hundred-fifty pounds to Agatha's average size for a five-year-old, something over three-feet tall, a corresponding weight), and motives that would be called controvertible. Agatha's contumely naturally increased but followed an intolerable period for them all, palpable silence, providing evidence, or the evidence, that Blinking Elvis's act had been not only inappropriate and brutal, but had been ineffective as well when she would show her contempt.

A period of tentative blows, as might be expected and seldom on the face after that and it made the girl lose any respect for Blinking Elvis, and her fondness was a thing of the past. Not to strike her would have been no worse but it seemed like it, the issue of the peas set a pattern that was impossible to break, Blinking Elvis, afraid of another overreaction or simply devastated by the first and the mother, could never regain that ideal balance, that has the effect of forging a bond between child and parent and could provide the means to correct errant behaviors, but in Agatha they went unchecked—again, because it would take a father who could but Blinking Elvis would reach out instead like a reflex sometimes, but never with the conviction that could command the necessary respect, and the fondness followed, both were lost.

Blinking Elvis was tired, a long time later and for an extended period he tried the same tactic on the mother, hitting, and measured waiting for the right moment when it seemed impulsive, an argument and saying something that would seem designed to enrage him. Naturally this didn't have the same effect as the child but it was satisfying in another sense, to relieve Blinking Elvis of certain tensions that would build up, pressure, but it didn't last long because the mother could leave, taking the by now teenage Agatha with her, as might be expected—Blinking Elvis didn't, or it didn't take him by surprise, for this and for other reasons only peripherally related to the issue of his habit of hitting them, his tendency to lock them out of the house for short periods, for instance, and he was not unaware that this contributed, as a part of something larger. If nothing else, Blinking Elvis was learning something about himself, in all the years with a wife and a daughter (one thing you could say about Blinking Elvis, he came to think of Agatha as his own daughter, and assumed he felt love, like a father could. Too bad there was no way she could have guessed, with all the hitting). But Blinking Elvis was not a bad man, evidence to the contrary notwithstanding, but hadn't learned appropriate outlets for emotional pressures, and still had to learn something about hitting, fortunately there was another opportunity.

Blinking Elvis struck a child a second time, this time his own son a number of years later, after Blinking Elvis had spent an unproductive and lonely period recovering from the loss of his

wife and daughter, and he remarried, this time to a younger
woman and no children of her own, or money. But for love
Blinking Elvis immediately got a job and became a model citizen,
not a model citizen but it was a respectable job, a clerk perhaps, or
a carpenter, but a job that could be secured by someone with his
talents and he could buy a house for his young wife, and the topic
of children, it didn't seem like a good idea but she was young and
it seemed like a good idea to her, she wanted to be a mother.
Blinking Elvis seemed changed by his years alone, and told his new
wife the stories of hitting and brutality but something was different, and seeing the difference and she said but a person can
change, Blinking Elvis didn't want kids now because he didn't want
to repeat the earlier behavior but finally she convinced him,
Blinking Elvis agreed to impregnate her (that sounds too clinical)
and of course nine months later she gave birth to a son.

The son, whom it will be convenient to call by his name,
which was Max, or Mike—it could be Mickey for short—and
would provide enough material for a book in itself, perhaps someone would care to take up this project. And for one year or two
years Max was simply or merely cute, and both parents found a
surfeit of opportunity for doting on him, as the saying is, and
weren't reluctant to indulge this habit. This is of course a common
enough pattern with new parents when one or both is young and a
first experience as an actual parent, and your own child makes all
the difference, the so-called biological link. I won't go into the
details. Because the issue of Blinking Elvis's relationship to Max,
and it turns out the basis of this relationship was indeed the child's
increasingly defiant behavior, which seemed to deliberately pro-
voke Blinking Elvis's choler, sometimes he was certain it did.
Example. Blinking Elvis couldn't understand how it was possible
that little Max, whom he appeared to love more than he could
explain, and in his toddling stage—all young children go through

this phase—it was barely possible to believe that the child was the issue of someone like Blinking Elvis, no one could ask for a son more ideal in every way, right down to his first words, which were not the usual da, or ma, but Blinking Elvis's own name, Blinking Elvis (there was a critical moment and Blinking Elvis feared his wife would be hurt or upset by these words—all parents, he knew, want their children's first words to be their own names, as if it would verify something. But the couple survived the crisis, partially due to Blinking Elvis's efforts to convince his wife that the child was actually uttering something about, "all of us." This is hard to believe. Nonetheless, and regardless, survived the crisis, and continued to enjoy a period of I won't say bliss), and for a time these remarkable, unbelievably touching incidents continued to counterbalance the negative effects of Max's periodic defiance, and relieved the parental anxiety caused by his willful acts of disobedience and deliberately urinating on the floor or doing the opposite of what he was told and when they would find bucket-fuls of dirt spilled out on the carpet, crayons can do a lot of damage but his smile, so like Blinking Elvis's own somehow, was enough to overwhelm them.

But on Max's third birthday things took a turn, when the little boy received a pair of new boots from his parents. Perhaps you can see what's coming. They chose them carefully both because they thought Max would feel proud among his neighbor-hood friends, sporting such fine haberdashery—there must be a better word than that when it comes to shoes, but they couldn't think of it—and because Max in fact needed boots for their weekly outings in the park, having grown to the point where he walked the whole way on his own steam. But why they chose the ugly brown ones, with all the lace-holes is anybody's guess, and something else that hadn't occurred to them, for Max immedi-ately found another advantage to having leather boots on his feet, so did they—from another perspective. Because the first time he was sent to his room—a form of discipline recommended by all the books—by, as it turned out, Blinking Elvis himself, for indulging his favorite forbidden ejaculation (i.e., NO), and stopping on the way by his father, who stood in a posture of authority, i.e., arms akimbo, long enough to administer a clumsy kick to the shin, enough to make Blinking Elvis bend down wincing to grab the spot with which Max had connected, while hopping up and down on the other foot (the pain was intensified by the sensitivity of a certain cloudy blemish—no doctor had been able to positively identify it—on Blinking Elvis's shin at the precise point Max's leather had met) made tears of pain come to his eyes and didn't know what to do.

We're nearing the critical moment: Blinking Elvis will soon be challenged with the promised chance to test his response to a situation that invites hitting, this must be set up carefully. Max's temptation to use his new boots as weapons was quickly discouraged by sending him immediately to his room, say. Or better, say by taking away a favorite toy whenever he threatened to repeat the attack—something, but something effective. Blinking Elvis and his young wife still had control of the situation, don't forget, but don't forget young Max's resourcefulness, kicking was not his only weapon, and the best tactic for challenging authority and the best way to claim independence, some things could be more frustrating to a parent, tantrums, but deliberately hurting yourself would have the most dramatic effect. Max learned that screaming, probably the single word no, while scratching his face with all four nails of each hand, hard enough to make marks and sometimes it would drive them to distraction, shaking him and growl to stop—even his mother—and then loving, a hug, and the idea love was missing. Riskier was hitting his head against the floor, and it hurt more but nothing was better to enrage his parents and

they were at a non-plus, Blinking Elvis was the enraged one but
they didn't know what to do. Now Max has them where he wants
them. And it began to seem to Blinking Elvis that there was no
solution, you can't let a child hurt himself, and doing it just to be
incorrigible or he wants to test your authority, limits and so on.
But what? You tell him to stop, talking to him rationally, or
affection, or if you ignore him, nothing within reason would
work, he would knock his brains out, the little shit. Love seemed
like it should be the answer, but this is where Blinking Elvis's
frustration was at its zenith, picking him up to hug him, give him
the love and forget the tantrum, etc., and the screaming increases
and, put me down, or go away and pushing him away is the
thanks he gets. But his wife said be patient, love is the right
response and eventually it will work out with enough patience,
and Blinking Elvis was determined to. Max got the better of this
strategy, though, and finally found a way to test Blinking Elvis's
patience and it was to the limit, love was out: Max hurt Blinking
Elvis, a three-year-old boy and actually and physically hurting his
father, the pain was severe, now he knew how Max felt knocking
his head against the floor because he picked him up to hug him
and so on and he knocked his head against Blinking Elvis's head,
a kind of wild thrash and made Blinking Elvis let him fall, sliding
down and on the floor and screaming, looking down and feels the
pain and the rage of it, being hit, raises his hand to strike and the
wife, screams Blinking Elvis!—and Blinking Elvis trembling and
his hand raised and trembling can't think, turns to the wife and
there are tears in his eyes, of pain, or she can't tell, frustration,
and running to Blinking Elvis and holds him and she sobs and
the boy on the floor, astonished by the effects of going beyond
certain limits.

The
Daughter

▼

THERE WAS A MAN who had a
daughter but he blamed his wife for the daughter, beautiful little
girl with pretty curls in her hair, two, almost three, but she
couldn't take a nap or she wouldn't take a nap and she didn't want
to go to bed and she wouldn't take no for an answer. It took an
hour, the man would lay with her or the wife would lay with her
and they had to sing to her the whole time, finally she would doze
off. The wife had insomnia and the man came to this conclusion
because of genes, he said. He didn't know if it was genes but the
daughter couldn't get to sleep, and the wife could never get to
sleep, it seemed like the wife. The daughter learned to pee in the
toilet but she would pee in her pants waiting until the last minute
and rush to the bathroom but sometimes she wouldn't make it in
time and she couldn't hold it—a habit of the wife's was to wait till
the last minute till she was squeezing her legs together—and
called it an accident as a little girl, she could already say quite a

few words and the man knew it was a sign of intelligence, also due to the wife's genes.

He had other daughters from four to sixteen but they didn't take after the wife's genes for some reason, but they had their own habits, they perhaps resembled each other, because they respected the older ones, envy was a factor, and they would imitate each other in a hierarchy. The man loved all these girls, of course, and he loved the wife, but he had a habit of seeming somehow each time to love the youngest best, for a period of a few years, as if he sensed a greater vulnerability when they were that young among the females in a family, and when a new girl was born each time the youngest would move up to join the sisters and the new daughter would get his attention and protection, his wife had the responsibility of menstruation. Allowance, and activities like gymnastics were equal and music lessons were equal. Music can stimulate memory like weather can, opening the window every year and you notice it's spring, it means a whole flood of memories from two apartments you lived in in spring before you were married, in two old houses in an area of the city, you remember spring-time there and certain events, reading in a chair and the evening breeze comes in, sex with girls who spent the night and wetness meant arousal as soon as you began to kiss each other. Or the other place, how the daylight lasts so much longer as the weather gets warmer and looking out the window at a lake in the park across the street, as dusk falls, would take your breath away, almost. Certain music is also associated with this second place, waiting for a phone call, waiting for a friend to come over.

But the new daughter meant spending too much time trying to get his daughter to go to sleep, and a nap was always an issue and every night was an issue with crying and defiance and he would get mad, struggling with his daughter because of resistance, and she had a mind of her own, a two-year-old and insisting on

the clothes she wanted to wear, dirty or not, and wouldn't wear
the appropriate shoes if it was raining or she wanted to wear
rubber boots if it wasn't raining. Or if she was tired: she wouldn't
ride in her stroller because she knew it meant falling asleep, or she
would scream I don't want to take a nap. This was a problem
because the man wanted authority and he would yell, and they
would scream at each other and made the neighbors wonder if
they should intrude sometimes or the man would yell at the other
daughters, because of his tension. He said get out of here before I
start yelling at you. The wife said you already started. The wife
said you're teaching her bad habits but the man said its your fault,
she knew he meant her genes but it pissed her off, because he
wasn't talking about her genes.

One day the man took one of his daughters to her cello lesson
on the subway and the wife had to go to a meeting and everyone
was busy, he had to bring the young daughter along, leaving some
extra time or she wouldn't have been able to come because she
always insisted on walking down the stairs at the subway station
herself—she could reach the handrail above her head now. If the
man was in a hurry he had to carry the little girl, and it would be
kicking and screaming because she wanted to be like the sisters
who were old enough to walk by themselves. The man avoided
it—she refused to hold his hand—except when there was time she
could walk alone or sometimes she would hold his hand and this
made it worthwhile. Of course the older daughter carried her
cello down the stairs, in its canvas case with a handle, and it took
her two hands but she could manage quite well, often she went
herself to her cello lesson.

They missed a train because of the slow walk down the stairs
but it didn't matter, the trains came quite often every ten minutes
and they knew this and they left themselves time for the slowness
of the little girl. Then, they were on the platform without a great

number of people because the train had just left but the man insisted his daughter hold his hand on the platform anyway, safety was a good policy even if no train was approaching and it was a rule he insisted on, she had to learn she had to accept it and she did, the alternative was to be carried, and if it was kicking and screaming it was up to her. The wife would let the daughter walk on the platform without holding her hand if there was no train coming and it made it worse but the man was firm, he said I'm not your mother. They sat on some chairs on the platform until the next train, and the little girl could stand on her chair and this was allowed, until the announcement was made that the train would arrive they got up and she had to take his hand. No stairs made a bus easier than a train and you didn't have to worry about safety so much, it was better to take the little girl on a bus if they could take the bus somewhere and sometimes the bus driver would talk to the man about his real interest, astronomy, because he subscribed to a science magazine, reading about the damaged Hubble Space Telescope when he took his break, at the end of the line where the man and his daughter got on the empty bus and the bus driver told him he was pissed that they would choose to put off repair of the telescope because they said the cost would mean canceling some silly shuttle missions, he couldn't see the value. He said he had been looking forward to fascinating new "images" (they aren't really images in the familiar sense of that term because what a telescope like the Hubble "sees" is really more like micro-waves)—but from unbelievably distant galaxies, which means from billions of years ago by the time the light reaches the telescope, and new theories about the big bang and the origins of the universe promised by the Hubble project. The whole thing was the result of some sloppy decision making— testing that could easily have been conducted at an earlier stage before the damn thing had been launched, but wasn't for some stupid bureaucratic reason or other—and now even the value of the advances that could be made was being questioned. He'd been following this project especially closely, and that was part of the reason, too, for his disappointment—he was excited when some unknown thing would turn up in one of these magazines, some previously unrecorded facts or images. But the man was surprised because the bus driver told him he was embarrassed about this interest, and experience told him there were two places he should hide it, when he went home and at the bus barn. It was like keeping *Playboy* under the mattress or it was like keeping *Playboy* in his lunchbox, a bus driver reading about the universe, he was glad to have the man to talk to, occasionally. He didn't expect his wife to share his interest but he remembered times in the past when she would seem to smile, or, why can't you watch tv with me when you get home, and relax together? At work it was sports. But the bus driver had a young son under four and it gave him hope because he said he hoped in a couple years the boy would develop a natural curiosity about science and the universe, etc., and he could begin to talk to his son about it and he would have someone to talk to, someday, and his son would share his passion for it like a companion.

The man and his daughters walked to the edge of the platform and stood behind the line, to wait. And eventually the train pulled up and the voice said some things about it on the loud speaker but it was scratchy and they couldn't understand what it said. It didn't matter because they read the sign above the door as the rickety subway train pulled to a stop and they knew which train to take and they were ready to get on when the doors slid open, the man was holding the little girl's hand but the other said, Dad—. He looked around and the cello was caught, in a hole in the platform so he turned to give her a hand but it was firmly in the hole, he had to reach down to the bottom where the cello was

stuck and pull hard and jerk, to get it out, and it came out
suddenly and the daughter took the cello and the man turned
back, to get on the train but the doors were almost closed and
tried to stick his foot out to stop the doors from closing but it was
too late, the little girl was on the train and he could see her
through the window, looking at him, there was a look in her eyes
and she didn't know what to do as the train pulled off. Neither
did the man, this had never happened to him before, even though
he had thought of the possibility. He wanted someone to tell him
what to do, his older daughter standing on the platform and he
wanted her to tell him what to do, he was worried this would
make her miss her lesson, but he knew it would—a lot of money
and it was a waste but it was irrelevant. His wife had the
responsibility of the money and paying the cello teacher but taxes
came and he told his wife to be more careful with the bills, she
said I don't have the luxury.

He looked but he couldn't find any transit police on the
platform so he went to the ticket booth, the trains go so fast and
she was past the next stop already, she was miles and miles away
already, but at the ticket booth they didn't think it was urgent, he
felt like he should grab someone by the shirt collar but they were
calling the transit police and he had to assume they were helping,
the man working in the ticket booth hung up when he saw the
nature of the serious problem from the man's face when the man
ran up to report his daughter, where he'd been talking on the
phone in the ticket booth to his young wife, because he knew he'd
have to phone the transit police immediately and it only took a
moment to say goodbye to his wife. They were talking about
what they could do to get a larger place than their small apartment in the city, it's all they could afford and maybe the man
would have to quit his job in the ticket booth so they could move
out of the city where the rent is reasonable, it would mean no job

but they'd just discovered the woman was not pregnant after all, but they thought she was, it was the second time they thought so, her period was really quite late, and the man made a confession when she finally got her period last week—hoped it turned out she had been pregnant and it made them both wonder if they wanted a child; she had forgotten to put in her diaphragm, and forgetting says something. There must be a way for him to continue going to college nights and they could have a baby, it wouldn't cost much because the woman could nurse the baby and they wouldn't have to spend as much on rent, they could move but the man had to hang up.

The woman was disappointed because talking to her husband about a baby before an emergency at the train, but she was alone in the apartment and she wasn't pregnant but she might be pregnant, soon, how did she feel about this? A baby nursing at your breast, or before that, in your body, a part of you and it comes out and then it's in the world but it takes awhile, nursing at your breast for what, a year? She had no idea. It sounded nice, but the responsibility grabbed her and it was something she'd have to talk to her friend about, and she wanted to talk to her husband when he got home, they had a lot of time or if they had different ideas about it and if they couldn't reach some decision there was even the possibility of finding someone else, a lot of life was left because they were young. She knew about possibilities and it made her reconsider, realizing a choice like that limits them but so does growing older no matter what choices you make. The young woman wanted to reassure herself about her possibilities, it was only the afternoon but she decided to make herself a drink, martini.

It seemed like they were on the phone to the transit police for a long time, just waiting, and the man was waiting, he looked around because he remembered his other daughter, but she was

standing nearby and she seemed worried but he didn't have to
worry about her, and her cello. His two-year-old daughter was
alone in the city somewhere alone on the subway—she was
almost three—and the transit police on the phone but how could
they find her, the next train was pulling into the station and
should he get on the train, he wondered if he could get down the
stairs in time, but what could he do? Nothing. Get off at the next
stop? It was impossible. He thought about his wife, and he
wished his wife was with them but he was afraid of what she
would think, because his wife knew he blamed her for the daughter and she would think he was careless because of resentment.
The wife would take the little girl's shoes off but she wouldn't
make the little girl put her shoes back on, later.

Finally the man came out of the booth and told the man to
take it easy because it was under control. He said have you found
her. The man said they hadn't found her, but the transit police
knew how to handle this kind of situation, it happened occasionally and there was a plan for alerting transit police at every station
and there would be someone at every exit to make sure someone
didn't make off with her. The man had thought of perverts but
this was the first time something like abduction occurred to him
and it terrified him, he asked and used the phone in the ticket
booth to call his wife.

His wife came to the station, where the man and their older
daughter were waiting, but before she arrived they found the little
girl, a lady brought her to a transit policeman across town, several
stops away. No one knew what she was doing for all those stops
or why it took her so long to reach the place where the lady
turned her in and of course she was too little to tell them, but
they asked her anyway but they couldn't make much of the
answers of a two-year-old. She got a ride in a transit police car
back to the station where her family waited, and she liked the

part about the police car but she was afraid of the policemen—
they can be friendly but it's the uniforms—and ran to the mother
and clung to her, she told the man later the little girl was just
trembling and it gave them a new perspective about their kids
on the subways, that the older girls wouldn't like, but it made
them realize how fragile it all was, lives and safety—but love,
and their love.

And that's how the man learned to be more tolerant of his
little girl's obstinacy, but for a long time the little girl couldn't
keep friends because she always had to have her way.

the phone was
G's ex-wife

▼

THE PHONE WAS G.'S EX-WIFE
and hearing a voice that he knew was the voice of his ex-wife
calling like a voice from a long distance from across the ocean she
said this is Jane, like it came from the past like a voice in a dream
from the past calling from the States it seemed to shock him
because he hadn't heard from his ex-wife in a long time, 6,
between 6 and 7 years, 10 years and didn't know how she got his
number outside the country the phones can be strange, there
must be a number you can call but Jane said the name Jane and
the assumption that he would know who was speaking was right
from the first moment she spoke across the ocean there was never
any question it was G.'s ex-wife's voice he heard the surprise of
hearing from her after all this time and the distance but the shock
of hearing the name and it was instantly her was more shocking,
or the voice and it was instantly her, but a struggle to overcome
the embarrassment of surprise and he didn't know what to say,

her name to get over the shock but to sound natural like he was
surprised to seem like he was glad he said *Jane* but he didn't know
what to add, that word *Jane* hanging in the air as they say G.'s ex-
wife didn't sound good with her "this is Jane" without a hello first
even without even asking G. his name as verification on the
phone gave her a tone of voice that sounded angry with bitterness
like a feeling that wasn't uncommon with her from the woman he
knew all those years ago, 7–10, like some other women feel a
similar anger he waited a short time and didn't say anything until
she said I'm not calling to say everything is a-okay he thought
that's one way to put it, but a difference in the words seemed like
a change from the self-righteousness of a woman of books on
power and women from the small sound of helplessness he could
hear in the words G.'s imagination said his ex-wife had no money
and had two girls and teenagers by now from another husband
before she was married to him there might have been a way she
could make him help her out if she could figure out how to with
what she needed because nothing would be different with a bad
situation with the girls' father G. knew he never contacted them
that Jane would call him to ask for something but asking G. in a
straightforward way would mean vulnerability would make it
unlikely because she must figure he'd offer something from guilt
if some maneuvering or some manipulation would make him
seem like part of it in a way the father wasn't, somehow, like she
didn't exist anymore and his daughters didn't exist for him anymore after she left him in Canada to go back to her hometown
he didn't exist for her either except as a symbol and he was, the
father but G.'s ex-wife had the responsibility of the kids and she
had to because no law could force their father to in Canada Jane
needed a symbol though and he could be a symbol or the symbol
can be a bridal in pictures G.'s seen Jane and her husband when
she was young smiling in a wedding picture with an expensive

gown and an armful of flowers that became a symbol of power-lessness in her world power began with the ability to see oppression in the fawning look on the bride's face in the picture holding her new husband's massive biceps, that she senses for the first time after the "festivities" and the close friends have gone home she would feel a difference when her pleasure in fucking is the same but some unpleasant change when he puts his penis inside her as *his wife* for the first time it will trouble her as she goes to sleep and would gradually become her anger and resentment would become power in her, it would help years later when she left her husband G. could be something else for awhile to take her side with sympathy and could work on life with her during those years, trying until finally it seemed to be *all* men when G. left she was aware of this idea of men when she told him to go both of them knew love had to be part of it though, and the daughters, it came up now in a way he had some money now from working and that could be interpreted as obligation but not a lot of money as a welder on oil rigs overseas to offer her anything she might need and G. was immediately on his guard but he had put a little away and you could say he was comfortable with a wife and little kids of his own G.'s ex-wife would call it his *second family* as if he had thrown *her* away but it was *her* and she knew her decision had been to turn her back finally on men and another marriage somehow it was him though when he came home once from a long trip sometimes he went to other cities looking for work as a carpenter or some kind of job he could work on after he came home he made a list of things for himself and bought some new tools or some tape to fix something before it got too dark he was anxious to do the things he liked in bed he liked his penis to get hard when he put his hands on his ex-wife's body she said you can't just come back and act like nothing has changed, he thought what *has* changed he was gone a long time G.'s ex-wife said everything isn't a-okay on the phone he said what's up, Jane said I have to ask you for something that told him it had to be something bad after hearing her say that she seemed about to come immediately to the point, but he didn't want to ask because he didn't want to know if someone was not-okay or someone was dead and the possibility of money kept him on his guard and knowing he had to think of something he could offer to take one of the girls now that he had a family of his own she might trust him to take a teenage girl to take off some of the burden of the money, but a problem of money was not the reason for her call she said I'm not going to ask you for money she said it was one of her daughters and Jane said it was her and her daughter Jane's expression on the phone was the fights are vicious, it sounded pretty bad from this word and from knowing Jane from being married to her someone could get hurt, not Jane if there were still guns in the house it could be Jane though with little kids in the house a gun in the house isn't dangerous because you can hide a gun effectively under the mattress like G.'s little kids wouldn't think to look under the mattress for his gun where he keeps it for his love because it defends his kids and his wife in a foreign country where so many people could be armed G.'s little boy rides a big-wheels in the narrow street and writes him messages that say I love you dad he wants to have a gun around like they had to have a gun where he lived with his ex-wife and her girls were little kids then on two occasions they used it in that neighborhood under the mattress once was a shadow but they bought two guns when one had a knife a gun could get involved in a fight like Jane described the viciousness when the police came when guns would go off in their neighborhood before it was about smoking dope Jane told him on the phone she said I find it in her room in the back of her dresser drawers in an obvious place Jane said she called the dope shit, she said I told her if she didn't stop smoking it she was out of here

Jane said it made G. think of another example of a friend and his outrage when his son got caught stealing a car he could sympathize when your kid puts himself or herself in danger and others in danger but he told his friend he didn't understand when he kicked the son out he didn't have a son G. told him he didn't agree with throwing away your kid from a feeling of rage Jane decided her daughter Jenifer would have to leave when she came home she found her and she found her so-called friend unexpectedly she said they were smoking marijuana in the backyard using a word like so-called says something about the friend but it means something about G.'s ex-wife and about her daughter, her affection for her daughter, because she said a fifteen-year-old can't go live with a bunch like that she said she can't stay here though using the expression fed-up Jane said she didn't know what to do, because finally there would be homes for juveniles but the implication that there was G. was in it from this story he understood Jane didn't smoke pot anymore like when they were married when her girls were little they would smoke it all the time and it didn't matter if her daughters were around there was nothing wrong with smoking pot like everyone then it seemed suddenly that it was evil, he couldn't say all of a sudden because 10 years is a long time to reverse your views on dope to the point of kicking out your daughter was hard to imagine though for someone who used to get stoned every day it made G. start wondering if he should believe her story about the dope but he asked himself if it mattered whether Jane kicked her daughter out because of dope or money or for some other reason a woman he knew simply farmed out her kids for a year to protect them from an abusive boyfriend because it would come to the same thing, the possibility that Jane's daughter would get on a plane to fly across the ocean to live with G. and his family made him realize he didn't want her story about dope to be true though he didn't want to have the problem of a teenager who smoked pot with little kids around the house it might have been an exaggeration G.'s ex-wife was using to get him to agree to something because all teenagers seem to smoke pot for reasons G. couldn't explain he'd been fond of Jane's daughter when he remembered her in day care and bringing her dolls to day care where she wasn't supposed to bring dolls, the kids at day care centers aren't as a rule allowed to bring their own toys and there are good reasons for a rule like this sitting at a very low table in a tiny chair with his knees up in the air where G. would bring her to school when her mother worked playing blocks on the low table before he had to leave, just right for the kids, the teenager Jane described was the same person apparently when G. heard his ex-wife on the phone and immediately he knew something would be required of him it was Jenny he thought of somehow to get out of it in a photo of this little girl her stringy hair was down to her shoulders that had been cut by her mother in a picture at day care looking down with seriousness and remembering it was a game of chess in the picture to cause the seriousness after a period of silence on the phone a good idea was asking something meaning-ful but something practical but fumbling from not knowing since he couldn't make himself ask directly about the situation he asked Jane if Jenny had graduated, the idea of her in pre-school and wondering about her later years in the so called upper grades but afraid to confront the immediate problem and not yet grasping it fully as they say he was beginning to understand what was re-quired of him she said an unhelpful word as an answer that meant G. was stalling for the deliberate reason that he was immediately again in a position of responding to the situation Jane said the word *yes* because it made no difference whether Jenny had gradu-ated and the reason that it made it seem like G. asking for the favor and Jane waiting with impatience like a person on a long distance phone call it was her money until finally he had to and

he said *what do you want me to do,* like they had always deferred
to the other in their talking to avoid responsibility or stall for her
or him to take the initiative when it had been a matter of a choice
between them she said a wife would always have to quit her job if
the decision was moving to another city where G. was offered a
job working as a shipbuilder it paid more but had to be too far for
her to keep a job she liked and the problem of day-care and the
problem of new friends was hard, he couldn't say she was wrong it
seemed like money was what G. had to think about though more
or less talking for a long time until a decision had to be made but
never admitting there had been no choice, or not that choice, the
amount of money a social worker made and the amount a day
laborer made the welding was a good wage though white arcing
light of the tip of a welding rod fusing together two pieces of solid
metal you can only look at its light through the black glass of a
welding hood if you don't know how you don't have an ever-so-
gentle touch to maintain the arc and that prevents the rod from
fusing itself instantly to the metal if it comes in actual contact it
has to be broken off to start again, no current means no bead but
when you do you keep the bead flowing and you can make a lot
of money knocking off the slag with a slag-hammer, more than
both of them put together it caused resentment like another
meaning in the words of talking about new plans for a house or
the difficulties of a mother sitting in a chair in emergency with
the baby in her arms Jenny was screaming from a deep cut the
woman with the form gave her a look like a bad mother but like
G. had some responsibility for a situation like this somehow sex
was love in their bodies but another meaning was in it too in bed
at night afterwards G.'s rough hand was on her white breast when
it was over it was over, G.'s ex-wife repeated his question by
reversing the pronouns of it to *what do I want you to do* again a
smallness in her voice that he didn't expect because repeating it

could have been but it didn't sound sarcastic like the past but like a plea it hit him the earnestness of love was in it and seemed like it was for her daughter that made her call him on the other side of the world to start him understanding a change from power to love in her he thought of her story of setting off in a broken down car with her little kids when she left her husband and Canada all those years ago with a leak in the gas tank for anger but it could be her love for her kids mostly, like G.'s own kids coming out after his wife pushing so hard with her face red from such a long time of trying to push a baby out of her body he could see a little bit of the head and thought there was some wet hair to see sometimes it would all go back inside her body though to start over telling his wife he saw the head like encouragement to open up her pelvis for a baby the doctor told her it was time to push again and again some breathing involving a rhythm would help with the pushing finally so much stretching the last time the baby didn't go back in, squeezing his wife's hand to tell her not to stop the bearing down it seemed like love came out with him even with the blood where G. saw too much stretching tear his wife's flesh apart between a woman and her child it would start off growing the whole time she was pregnant to be there forever, like G.'s ex-wife calling him for the sake of her daughter he saw there was responsibility involved and it was his and his love and what he had to do he said let me call you back for the second time in 10 years he called his ex-wife by her name he said let me call you back Jane I'll have to work out some things, a couple days.

John's Habit

▼

NIGHTTIME, and stopping in
front of a house where girls lived because the father was the father
of girls and had been John's friend of other times. He didn't
remember how he got there, driving with his son in the car John
suddenly found himself in front of the big house. His son might
like to play with the girls but he said he didn't want to, but he
would like the big house if he decided not to play with the girls,
John said one was his age, but there would be old things in the
house and a big house of interest to "explore." John didn't know
if his son was too old to "explore," a tall and morose boy and now
it had been a number of years since the times of discovering his
son with dried dirt around his mouth and stuck to his lips from
eating mouthfuls of earth in a youthful way, or didn't know if his
son was too old to "play." When he would see his son he was
trying to reach his arms around the rough bark of a large tree, or
he placed his face against the cement blocks of a high wall, John
didn't consider these things to be playing. No streetlights and a

dark night in the dry desert, weeds sticking up and occasional piñon trees bent at an angle, then a sudden drop-off and the city sprawled below, seemed more noticeable, the lights must have represented so many buildings and gave John pause to think of it and the people in them. He walked across the front yard with his son toward the door and John turned his attention to the boy: the last time we were here, he said do you remember the house or the girls? He knew the boy didn't want to seem interested, at that age it was probably the time of the rebellion of his body and the idea of girls, he said something to his father that sounded bored, and made John feel peevish from inadequacy inside from trying to reassure his son, reminding him that they were older, like he was, he thought he could influence him with this information but his son was unimpressed. Well, the house then, and the son conceded that a massive house might be good, with junk already on the front porch.

It reminded John of junk from last time and some things added color like a rescued traffic signal hanging as a flashing porch-light and gave John a familiar feeling and made him glad to have a friend who would have the things scattered around and evidence of the daughters. A long time ago the mother died, he couldn't remember if he had told his son this or if he knew, he decided if he was puzzled he would ask, though, or could ask, by his age a kid would figure it out, because these things happen, and the circumstances of his own mother could be another reason, he didn't think it was important to go into it with him now. They both looked around and looked at the things on the porch and the son paused to scratch himself, John must not have noticed or he decided not to pay attention, he would have said something. An enormous old wooden door on hinges, just then it swung open into the house and the friend, leaning on his crutches with his empty pantleg folded up underneath as usual, and

pinned, he had a cigarette butt between his lips unlit from before
and was smiling his warmest smile, because he hadn't seen John
and his son for some time, although they went back to childhood
they had different lives. John's silver Zippo, worn down by years
in his pocket, and John offered a flame from it to the friend for
the stump of a cigarette in his mouth and made the feelings come
back like it always did, the same feeling of an oasis in their lives or
a respite in their lives to go back and to see something in their
kids, fathers without wives and you share something.

His son stood with him while he shook hands with his friend
and they patted each other's shoulders, etc., and the daughters
in the background, noticing their presence but somewhere in
another room, girls like that would do homework or play a
musical instrument, but a situation that wouldn't encourage the
son to leave his father and made him impatient to sit in a room
with the two men. It might be interesting to listen to them
talking, he hadn't thought about it but it seemed like he would
have to. John could tell part of him wanted to go with the girls
from the boredom of a parent, like resentment, and he wanted to
do something to help his son with this but what. Nothing. He
went with his friend into the big room that made him think of
the term "gallery," cluttered with things and dust, and they all sat
on three chairs of an old house. John wanted to give his attention
to his friend but his son was a problem, thinking they might but
the girls didn't do anything to solve this problem, they stayed out
of sight somewhere in the background and couldn't be heard, or
he wondered if his friend would call his daughters. He knew he
wouldn't though, because his friend wasn't the kind of parent to
force them to do something and the delicacy of a single father
would prevent it, or should prevent it. It seemed like there was
nothing to be done, hoping something would happen and the son
could explore the house, he turned his attention to his friend.

He was already talking about something that would solve the dilemma of John's son, he said he wanted to show him something. John thought this included his son but the friend told them he would talk to his daughters and they agreed to join John's son, pulling himself up with grace hanging from his crutches he told John there was something to show him, not a room but no other word for it seemed adequate so he asked his daughters through their door and both appeared, ready to accommodate with a look of eagerness John couldn't interpret, it was unexpected from his memory of them, he didn't know what to think. He looked at his son but the turn of events aggravated the son's moroseness to be with the girls but there was no alternative but he glanced at his father as he walked off with his friend on crutches, John saw the glance.

He turned to his friend then and asked his friend, he admitted there was no other word for it than a room but it was through a tunnel and that seemed to make all the difference. John didn't see how it could but his friend explained that the structure of the original house, the builders and the idea of a hallway, something had to be done and the tunnel solved it. Then somehow it had turned out to be more than that. One leg was no problem because years of practice since losing a leg meant John's friend could crawl through something like a tunnel with his crutches in one hand, crawling on a substance of roughness like burlap but a substance that covered something like soft rubber finally a short distance through the tunnel, ten feet, the room, small, dim and made John think of the term "chamber." It is a chamber said the friend and said but there's something else, and another reason to show you the room, he saw John's anxiety. For this "chamber" was the place they could resolve the conflicts of "wives," the friend already knew this from his daughters and his eagerness was to share something with John and another single father: his own

wife died whereas John's wife had left, but the problem of "a wife"
was there nevertheless, it affected him and it affected his daughters. He explained to John that the room had changed all that, the
daughters' previous hostility and he told him I noticed your son's
moroseness and these are the consequences of "a wife," the resentment of no mother that could never be explained, because he told
John of a small niche or recess for a shelf left when the builders
had carved the room out, and a chair by it and John's friend would
sit whispering into the small recess the silences of a marriage and
those things you couldn't tell your daughters with no one to
confide in had created the conflict John remembered between his
friend and his friend's daughters. He said it was resolved in the
room to simply say the things but all the things you couldn't tell
your children, the idea of a pressure valve John's friend said, you've
tried something similar from the pressure on you walking in the
desert, maybe a cold night with stars or after your wife was gone,
in the desert at night and revealing the pain of a marriage to the
stars that you could never tell your son because the pleasure you
had in him from love always seemed to accompany the pain or
intensify the pain. You can find the relief you couldn't find in the
cold desert though and you can find it in the recess.

John's friend finished saying these things and he got up
between his wooden crutches swinging a step at a time he made
his familiar way across the low room now, John watched him and
he "lowered himself" into the comfortable chair of the recess,
a hollow in the rough wall of the corner of the chamber. His
friend began to whisper something and it was apparently the
silences, John didn't see how it could be but the friend seemed to
be speaking and it was the feeling of being heard, listening for a
short period in thought before a brief nod would seem to repeat
something already said, in a different register perhaps, and understanding is achieved. John stood watching for a long time,

it seemed like a long time wondering and finally seemed like the friend had forgotten he was in the room, his friend had forgotten but remembered and a content look of satisfaction on his face turning saw John immediately rose from the comfortable seat and urged his friend to take his spot, when he whispered the silences of his "wife" he'd begin to feel the pressures of a father relieved, said his friend.

John naturally was skeptical but an old friend of other times and something in him trusted his friend, he told himself the other had gone first after all and began to wonder if he had been seeing the effects in the easiness of his friend and his blue eyes and John's earlier confusion of the daughters' compliance. He sat down on the chair and began to whisper into the recess, he murmured secrets before only revealed to some desert aloneness, as his friend put it, or a shout but silent like a whisper like the rage of everything she had inside and his wife would let a boy like their son suck it, and suck until she would give all of it to a child, milk, but it must be blood and everything inside. The friend had been right and John thought he felt something like satisfaction, no sound coming back but speaking into the recess in a whisper and you felt as if there was a listener for the first time perhaps, he lost track of his friend as he whispered certain silences of a "wife," John said or he might suck on his wife and when he could there was a small sweetness from his infant son but it seemed to be an emptiness, his wife told him she felt abused from so much sucking but John didn't understand, he said he could never understand what seemed to be natural. Finally a look on his face like relief like his friend and recalling the other's presence, then standing in uncanny gratitude and the friend on his crutches watching for John's reaction, nothing to be said. The friend said but the tunnel is where a feeling of satisfaction can be sealed, to go back through the tunnel sets real changes, they crawled back through the tunnel into the bright light of the big house, rough but the feeling of soft rubber beneath your knees and the shock of another world coming through.

His son was obviously glad it was over back out in the night-time and the city lights below, but surly now as ever, pissed, his father was the reason. To leave him alone with the girls. John was thinking about his ex-wife and the good feeling of the satisfaction of the chamber and the recess, though, he didn't want to acknowledge this moodiness of his son, he said you could have explored the big house, he said get in the car. They were walking in the desert moonlight across the friend's yard on the way to the car and the boy saw a slow turtle, he picked it up and his father saw him take it to the edge of the drop-off and heave it down into the city lights below for the sake of his rage, like sometimes a boy will destroy a living thing smaller than himself as a sign.

JOHN COULD COME BACK, naturally, his friend, and a new habit was visiting his friend, for the first time he could reveal the silences of his marriage in that dim chamber, some of them, built into the earth of the friend's big house in a roughed-out hollow left by workmen as a shelf, perhaps. For John the pleasure and the relief of the first night repeated and intensified in subsequent visits, deepened, and the friend said you'll begin to notice the differences in your son or the change of a rebirth for you, it will make a difference in your son, his friend said emerging from the tunnel you'll feel it. John didn't say anything about his son and he didn't care about the tunnel though, it was the dim room and it was the recess and it was his silences to his "wife," or it was re-hearsing the petty secrets of a marriage, he said he called his wife to tell her he'd be home late because of work, she was pissed but it was work and it was consideration, he said cellophane was on the bathroom floor, for days from a tampax wrapper and it was until he picked it up but John said his small son was fussing and screaming, it seemed like screaming from being alone with John, screaming because of his hunger so he put his finger in the little boy's mouth and he sucked but nothing came out for his hunger until his wife came home with her tits. John would visit his friend and he didn't know if his friend would but John would whisper the silences of his "wife" and his friend was right, it was being heard and it was a release. John said no sex made itself worse, like any other problem if something else prevents you from confronting it until you get that resolved, having it even when sex was awkward was something they couldn't have forced themselves to do though, like talking, because their sex had been sucked out with everything.

John was different from the room and his son noticed a difference but it was worse, and John's friend noticed something in John, it was the difference of an addict. John's anxiety could only be relieved by murmuring his silences into the roughness of the plaster recess to get a good feeling, he said a kid wants to know the right way to spell something if he's four, what's wrong with telling him, because you always give him the message everything he does is right and he's not going to reach out, beyond you, why should he. A theory said you just tell the kid he spells it and it's right like your milk for his hunger.

He went every week but he had to go every night and his son was sullen, a boy and the confusion of his blood and his puberty made this natural, but he had to come with his father and made it worse when the girls were home, but it was the struggle with his father, he said I'm staying home tonight. John didn't want him to stay home but he wanted to go to his friend's, he told his son to go to his own friend's house but without asking the parents and if they objected it would be a shame and maybe John should apologize. He didn't apologize though, but he went without his son and this became another habit and the boy didn't like to but it was better staying with his friend when his father went without him, it seemed like he was a drunk and seemed like the parents thought he was a drunk, they let John's son come to their house and they didn't say anything. John didn't like this situation of his son very much but he wanted to go to his friend's house and his friend's chamber where he could whisper the things from his silences to his wife from his memory and would make him feel good from it, he said something was missing because everything finally must have gone into his wife from her mother's thin body, sisters were the same, but it meant everything would have to flow through her tits and their tits with their milk and to their small kids, John could never correct this bad habit of a family like her sullen father said nothing was left. But whispering it would draw up more of the unsaid from the well of him after the silences were whispered, the anxiety released was immediately replaced from so many of his unspoken things of his marriage, to make a marriage finally impossible. He already wanted to come back to his friend's house whenever he left to climb the steps to the porch and the blinking traffic light, through the tunnel and the recess in the wall could make him feel good, there was no way to say how good. John's friend saw his need of an addiction but his concern was a conflict with John's need, the whispering was what mattered like nothing else, John said mind your own business.

I T WAS A LARGE TOWN but John's son's friend's parents raised a number of rabbits in cages in back of their house, and sometimes neighbors would buy one to eat. John's son's friend's father called to them, he said come out into the backyard, hurry. They ran and a rabbit was giving birth, it was something the father

thought the boys should see as a life-lesson. They thought it was
disgusting but it was wonderful to see the little wet rabbits with
their eyes glued shut being finally squeezed out into the light and
the world. John's son's friend had seen it before of course, but
John's son was glad he had the opportunity and now he knew
something about birth. Later that day John's son and his friend
came out the back door into the cold Fall afternoon and they saw
his friend's father, he held a squirming white rabbit up by the feet
and John's son saw him swing an iron pipe and the thud of it
on the rabbit's skull. He liked it when his friend's mother fried
rabbit for dinner.

Douglas Gunn

was born in Albuquerque, New Mexico, in 1950. He has since lived in and around St. Louis, Denver and Idledale, CO, Binghampton, NY, and Philadelphia. For the last three years he has lived in Tokyo where he teaches at Temple University Japan. He has been a cabinet maker, a deck-hand, and a shipyard worker. His first collection of stories is *and working* (Permanent Press, London, 1991).

Author's Statement: One of my chief interests as a writer is finding ways to allow various perspectives and voices to overlap and invade each other. Many of my stories rely on intrusions in the form of various subtitles, or interruptions and frames tangential to the narratives, which organize the content according to different, often conflicting perspectives. In others my intention is more specifically to violate the boundaries of the unitary self and its linguistic counterpart, the sentence, which I try to accomplish by overlapping the syntax of the narratives, in more or less dramatic ways. The focus, in these stories, is on interrupting and disrupting the language itself of the single, unified perspective. Others are interrupted only by the syntactical distractions of the narrators, distractions which convey the dilemmas of characters whose worlds don't square with the official ideology condensed in conventional language.

The "content" I find most compatible with these concerns with language: working-class characters, the citizens of unofficial America confronted with authority in its many forms; the anxieties and dilemmas produced by the disparity between the instability of their lives and the coherence of everyday language. No "solution" is suggested, beyond the attempt to release these characters into the always new and unsettling present by disrupting the official language that defines the only reality available to them.

Any summary of my intentions like this one is bound to be inadequate, and I always end up feeling like it does an injustice to the stories; in the end, they have to speak for themselves no matter what. My own description of my fiction is bound to be skewed.

▼